Witches Hill

First published by Mogzilla in 2016

Paperback edition:
ISBN: 9781906132255
Text copyright Jon Chant

Cover ©Mogzilla 2015

Printed in the UK

http://www.mogzilla.co.uk/witcheshill

Witches Hill

by

Jon Chant

MOGZILLA

Chapter zero

Stop me if you've heard this one: a city kid, sent
to visit a relative in the countryside, and when I got
there, my magical friends and I had an adventure with a
talking dog and a girl.

It didn't go the way you think.

It all started when my grandmother got a text.

My grandmother's good like that. She's also the
Archmage of Time.

Our flat is sparse, and the windows are too small.
Abuela doesn't like having too many things. The
wallpaper came with the flat, since the walls are ancient
and we're not allowed to disturb them. The furniture is
stuff that people have given or bought for us over the
years, and none of it matches: we have an old walnut
sideboard full of books, the TV sits on a cheap white
plastic table and the couch is a hyper-modern red thing
from the 80s.

She looked at herself in the mirror, ready for a day
of being avoided by everyone, when her phone chirped.
It's an old Spanish tune from when she was young. I
had to find it and help her put it on there. She picked up
her phone and stared at it in mild offense.

I carried on gaming, at least until I felt the chill of
her gaze resting on me.

"Abuela?" I asked, pressing pause on the game.

(I should explain: Abuela's Spanish for grandmother, since my grandmother is Spanish.)

She looked through me, her brows pinched into a knot.

"Your Aunt Vanessa," she said, and put the phone on the sideboard. "A message."

A pulse of excitement went through me. I don't go to school, so I spend a stupid amount of my time here behind four walls.

"What does she want?" I asked.

Abuela gave me a none-too-secret smirk.

"She wants you because you are not me. She needs one of us because she has a problem with time," Abuela said. She picked up the phone again and read off the screen. "She says: 'there is a ghost...but you are too busy for this, Mama, so please if you could send Esteban, that would be wonderful...'"

I tried not to show too much enthusiasm. Abuela smiled. Her face is thin and sharp. She smiles as if she has an axe hidden behind her back.

"Where is Aunt Vanessa?" I asked.

Abuela's eyes narrowed with the effort of remembering.

"North," she said. "She digs holes."

"Oh," I said. "Right."

Abuela smiled again.

"I think you should go," Abuela said. "It will be good for you. Your Aunt likes to be outdoors. You spend too long staring at that screen; it's a terrible strain for a helpless old woman."

"Shall I book a train ticket?" I asked, reaching for my laptop.

"A train ticket? A train ticket?!?" Abuela said, her eyes blazing with indignation. "You are my apprentice, you will travel by magic. Speak to your friends. Tell Daniel there will be bicycles. I will speak to the other if she will not come. The outside will be good for them."

My stomach sank. I do sometimes wonder if I did bad things in a previous life.

"Ghosts?" I asked. "What can I do about that?"

My grandmother flashed a knowing smile, and shook her head.

"No," she said. "That is for you to decide. Find out when you get there."

Chapter One

So... my name is Esteban Fawkes and I'm a sorcerer.

There are different kinds of magic: some of it's like trying to learn the guitar, you just practise until you get it right. Some of it's like being able to roll your tongue: either you can or you can't. That's the kind of magic I've got. I'm a Chronomancer, so I control the magic of time.

We arrived in an empty field on a rolling hill. There was grass in both directions as far as you could see. An empty road cut across the brow of the hill, running next to the field, and the valley had a town off in the distance.

The air ripped open and a fiery circle appeared on the grass. A gigantic bird-man-creature appeared in a circle.

The bird thing is Medimiel. He works for my best friend Danny. Danny's the tall mixed race guy falling out of the circle. I'm the short, fat kid with the curly hair. I'm a year older, not that you'd know to look at me. Danny's tall, smart, and good-looking. He hits the ground, rolls, and makes it to his feet. I just roll.

One more person steps out of the circle. It's lucky there aren't any cars on this road. No matter what they thought they'd seen, they'd remember Connie: she's tall with bright white hair. She steps out of the circle as if she's getting off an escalator, but she doesn't trip or roll. She's got one hand holding an oversized handbag and the other clamping a pair of huge, black shades to her face.

Reality closes and the flaming circle vanishes, leaving only Medimiel, scorched grass, and us. Danny managed to jog to a stop, and gravity finished rolling me down the hill, which Connie watched with a guilty little smile. She gives Danny a sideways glance and he tries to pretend he's not out of breath.

"Yeah…" Danny said. "Well… you've had more practise than me."

Connie tried to stop laughing. It sounded like something between a snort and a hoot.

"Don't laugh, he's right," I shout over from where I've landed. "When I'm your age, I'll probably stop falling on my face all the time."

Connie nodded and managed to stop the obvious smirking.

Danny does creatures, 'Things That Should Not Be Here' as we call them. Connie's an alchemist… and, in a way, she's a 'Thing That Should Not Be Here' too. It's a long story.

"Sorry boys," Connie said; her body still shook with laughter. "It was a good first attempt."

Connie doubled over, gripping her shades to her face.

"Oh dear..." she giggled.

"Yeah, well," Danny said, helping me to my feet. "We got here."

"Where is 'here?'" Connie asked.

Abuela had given Danny all the locations and addresses, since he was the one casting the travel spell. He looked it up on his phone.

"Yeah, Hobb's Field, Pendle Forest, Lancashire," Danny said.

I looked around the site. There weren't many trees: just rolling hills and fields as far as the eye could see. I could see towns and villages in the distance.

"This doesn't look much like a forest..." I said.

Connie shook her head.

"Forest is a Medieval title. It just means an area where people were allowed to hunt," she said. "I wish someone had told me I was going to be in Pendle."

Danny gave her a suspicious look.

"Why?" he asked.

Connie didn't look happy. You couldn't always tell the expression behind her huge shades, but I'd have to have been blind not to see she was worried.

"It's probably nothing," she said.

Connie's good at not bothering to tell us things. When it comes to actual lies, she's terrible. Danny raised an eyebrow.

"Doesn't sound like nothing," he said.

Connie waved him away, searching around for something. She walked in a small circle, checking the grass as if it was the most interesting thing in the world.

"Yeah, I've got to be honest," I said. "You look like you want to murder someone."

"Don't worry," Connie said, looking around with more of an urgent sense. "It's just some stuff that happened before I was born."

Danny gave me a look. That's a long time ago. Connie was born in the 1650s.

"That—" Danny started to say.

"Have either of you noticed we don't have our bags?" Connie said.

Danny played it cooler than me. Also, because he's a conjurer he knew it wasn't worth looking. We'd just used the magic of a bird-angel to travel from London to Lancashire in forty-five seconds. If the bags weren't here, we were never seeing them again.

"Great. Would it be pointless asking where they are?" I asked.

I looked around anyway, hoping my backpack would be somewhere in the long grass.

Danny peered into the middle distance and put his hands in his pockets.

"Let me put it this way…" he said. " We all move on to the next world. When you do, you'll see your phone and laptop again."

I kicked a lump of earth. My laptop. It wasn't fair to blame Danny, but I did anyway.

"Smooth," I said. "Brilliant conjuring. Well done."

"I didn't do it. I conjured Medimiel. The book says he can 'transport ye fast from one place to another."

Danny jerked a thumb at Medimiel, who had started to preen his feathers. I do sometimes wonder if he really knows what's happening. Then again, we're ants to him. I don't know much about the emotions and dramas of ants, or how they feel about losing ant-

luggage.

"What was Connie saying about a 'new friend', anyway?" I asked. "Something tells me she doesn't mean Anil from the shop."

Danny smiled his 'I'm so brilliant' smile and shook his dreads.

"Nah," he said. "I've been talking to a new angel. Lunariel. He's dodgy though."

I gave him a look and then glanced at Connie. She folded her arms and turned away.

"It's alright," Danny said. "I know how to do it and I know the rules. It could be years before I give him the kind of things I've given to Medimiel."

"Okay," I said, still not happy. "And the luggage is gone. Time for my next trick. I need to test time."

Danny shrugged and Connie looked doubtful, but neither of them understands what I do. Most trained sorcerers don't fully get time magic.

"I've got to do it before I do any Chronomancy. It's like testing the ground before you jump up and down on it," I said. "Since Auntie Vee didn't invite me here to drink tea."

Danny shrugged. He managed to at least look sorry for losing our stuff.

"Fair enough mate, we'll wait here," he said.

I took a deep breath. I can pull things back and forward in time – objects, people and that sort of thing – but the only way to test an area for the first time is to travel myself. Connie watched me with the same expression she'd had since she realised we were in

Pendle.

I threw myself back in time. Just as I was about to disappear, Connie's face turned to a look of horror.

"Esteban, look at that!" she said, and tried to grab me.

I lost my grip on time and fell back into the present.

We weren't on our own anymore: three figures had appeared.

"Well," I said. "I said there would be ghosts..."

Chapter Two

I bet people walking through Hobb's Field have reported seeing ghosts: moments leaking out of time. That's how most ghosts work: just recordings set off when people disturb time.

Angry voices and shouting cut the air. A woman screamed. I reached out with my magic and tried to steady the ripples in time. The blue skies disappeared behind lead grey clouds.

We definitely weren't on our own in the field. Three men walked through, with linen sacks slung over their shoulders. They looked like they worked on the land. Their clothes weren't bad, but they were rough and worn. The other one, the youngest, was better dressed. His shoes didn't look like they were used to having mud on them.

"Look father," said the youngest man. "She's a witch."

The man coughed. It was a nasty cough – sharp and wet. It made him shake for a minute. His breath whistled in and out, and he shook his head.

"Mind yourself, I'll have no talk like that," he said, after he'd recovered his breath.

The younger man looked at the one in the middle – who looked the right age to be an uncle or an older brother – but the other man stayed gloomily silent.

I took a deep breath. Time was settling down again

and I could feel the present tugging at them. Not hard enough to send them home — yet.

The men got closer. Danny gave me a sidelong look and put his hands into his pockets. Conjuring takes a very, very long time, but these days he always keeps something prepared.

"Are we going to have to talk to them?" Danny asked. "I don't fancy explaining myself to someone who likes to throw around the word 'witch.'"

The oldest man looked straight through me. The youngest, a youngest son by the look of him, didn't even look in my direction. The other man, an older son, looked at me and frowned.

"Come and speak to Master Newell," the youngest said. "There's ways of checking."

"Not a word of it," the old man said, between coughing. "They're a bad lot, but I won't have them tried as witches. Get along."

"Malkin Tower is full of witches, I heard—" the younger man started.

"You shut your trap," the old man said.

The father still looked straight through me. They were almost standing next to me.

I turned to Connie and smiled.

"Don't worry," I said. "We're alright. They're like a tape recording. They might talk back to us if we made an effort, but they wouldn't understand we're not supposed to be here."

"They say the old woman killed that cow—" the youngest continued.

"Rubbish," the old man said, between coughing. "You've got me going now. There's no such thing as witches. There's a young girl down in that house. I won't have it."

"But father—" the youngest said.

"No. You go off with Sir Richard to the Assizes. When you get back you'll be in better mind."

"I don't know, father…" the brother said, waving an arm in front of him. "There's something wrong with that family, and that house."

The old man swore and picked up a stone.

"You're both daft," he said, and brushed the dirt off the stone.

He was sick, but he wasn't weak. He wound his arm back and threw the stone as hard as he could. The stone flew straight and true.

It hit me, or at least it flew through where I was. It went straight through my chest, out the other side and landed on the grass without hurting me.

"Ow," I said, more out of habit than because I felt anything.

The stone vanished from the 21st century grass. Then the men vanished as well, along with Medimiel. Danny and Connie scrambled towards me.

"Blooded Nails, are you alright?" Connie asked.

She reached over and grabbed my injured shoulder.

"It didn't even hit me, to be honest," I said. "That was cool."

"So… time's quite weak here, is it?" Danny said.

"Well done Sherlock," I said. "It happens a lot

outside of big cities, though."

"Looks like it banished Medimiel," Danny said. "If we're lucky he might find our stuff."

Connie cleared her throat. She had her phone in her hand.

"Look at your watches," she said.

Neither of us had watches. Who needs a watch when you've got the time on your phone?

Unfortunately, my phone was now lost in the vortex of time. We crowded around Connie's phone to see what the time was. Danny gave a low whistle.

"Look at that," he said. "We've lost an hour."

A note of excitement entered Danny's voice.

"There's a text though," he said. "Your auntie's here with the bikes."

"Oh. Joy." I said.

My face must have been a picture. Connie's face lit up into a smile, despite the look of worry since she'd known we were in Pendle.

"I'm sorry," she said, snorting involuntarily. "But I can't wait to see you ride a bike."

A Land rover came around the corner with four bikes strapped to the back. My auntie Vanessa backed into the field and jumped out, her explosion of curly black hair tied back behind her head.

I sometimes wonder if my grandmother and auntie Vanessa are actual relations: I've seen Abuela smile exactly five times, and one of those was just after I stopped a demon from stealing London.

Auntie V is a tiny grinning ball of energy. She's only

just taller than I am.

She jogged up to us, her face split from ear to ear with a smile.

"Here we go: get the bikes down, I'll park up, and we can ride the rest of the way to the cottage."

"Sweet…" said Danny.

He started to set up the bikes after unclipping them from the rack.

"I don't know what you three are up to," he said. "But this is how I'm spending my weekend."

Connie raised an eyebrow.

"How are we spending our weekend?" she asked.

"Hasn't anyone told you?" Aunt Vanessa asked. "We've uncovered a witch's cottage. You're here to get rid of the ghost."

Chapter Three

Malkin Tower was a cottage outside the village of Newchurch. Originally, it had been a stone cottage with a thatched roof. It did look like a tower – tall and narrow. The walls were black from weathering and the house didn't look like it had ever had any glass in its windows. You could see where the shutters were attached a long time ago, but the wood must have rotted away.

The roof was long gone too, after hundreds of years of Lancashire weather. I don't know how long ago it last rained, but the ground was still muddy.

We'd cycled all the way here from the hill. Danny had loved it, Connie had put up with it, and I felt like I was going to explode. After we had some minor trouble with the Great Fire of London, I promised myself I was going to get fit, but there are many good films in the world, and they weren't going to watch themselves.

Danny looked back, effortlessly dismounting his bike while it was still moving.

"Are you alright, mate?" he asked.

I nodded, which was a lie. The last time I was this out of breath, I was being chased by a fire spirit.

"I can't believe I just did that for no reason."

Aunt Vanessa laughed.

"Come on, we needed to get to the cottage," she said.

Connie got off her bike more carefully, holding her shades onto her face as she did. She'd been adjusting them every two minutes since Vanessa had appeared.

"Esteban doesn't do exercise unless someone's trying to destroy him," Connie said.

"We'll see about that," Vanessa said. "I'm sure I can find something he'll enjoy."

My eyes were streaming and I could hardly breathe. I got off my bike gracelessly, skidding in the mud so that I almost fell over, and stared at her.

"We might try flatter ground, though," Vanessa said. "It'll be nice so long as the weather holds."

I followed Danny into the cottage. It was only one room, but there were post-holes where wooden beams had supported another floor upstairs. There wasn't much left. Plastic bags and bits of rubbish had blown in over time. There were a few rotten bits of wood in the corners, but that was about it.

"So this is the witches' cottage?" I asked.

Aunt Vanessa gave me the look people always give me when I know something I shouldn't. This is why I try to only hang around with sorcerers.

"You said it about ten times," I said. "Don't look at me like that."

"Have you looked back at what it used to be like?" Danny asked.

I started to answer him, but I realised he was talking to Vanessa. Her smile faltered.

"Ah. I'm not a Chronomancer. I'm the only one in the family who didn't get it. I'm an archaeologist," she said.

"Have you run any tests?" Danny asked, without missing a beat.

Vanessa smiled and nodded, trying to recover her good cheer.

"The cottage is around four hundred years old, and there's no cellar. We can tell that humans lived here, not sheep or cows, but that's all we have," she said.

"That's older than Connie," Danny said.

"Don't be cruel," Aunt Vanessa said, frowning.

"Yes," Connie said. "A lot of things are older than me."

"Yeah," Danny said. "Mountains, forests, glaciers…"

"So, what do you want us to do?" I asked, trying to steer the conversation away from a path that led Danny into pain.

Aunt Vanessa hesitated. Her smile was sincere, but uncertain.

"Well, first I'd like to get rid of the ghost. Then, if it would be alright, I'd like to set up a magical archaeology lab. Just for the weekend. You can look back in time here and survey what happened, and whichever one of you is the alchemist can test things for magic. I want to know if the witches here were sor–" Aunt Vanessa started.

"They weren't." Connie snapped.

Aunt Vanessa kept smiling.

"Well now, it's not that sim–" she started saying.

"They weren't," Connie snapped again. "I know:

I saw the witch trials. I was there. They were mad people, and they were poor people. Sometimes they were people who weren't that nice, but not one of them ever did magic."

Vanessa looked at Connie, frowning.

"You'd have be–"

"I'm three hundred and sixty-three years old. People didn't accuse sorcerers of witchcraft. We're too useful. Everyone who ever found out I was an alchemist just wanted me to turn lead into gold."

"Okay, but we still have to look for evidence. That's how archaeology works," Vanessa said.

Connie frowned and crossed her arms, but didn't say anything.

"So, anyway… if you're the alchemist you can use my kitchen. It's got heat and water, unless you need something else," Aunt Vanessa said.

Connie shook her head.

"No," she said. "That's everything. Sorry."

Aunt Vanessa patted her shoulder.

"No, it's alright. You must have been frightened."

"They weren't always good people but they shouldn't have died," Connie said.

Danny raised an eyebrow.

"Doesn't sound like they were much of a loss," he said.

Connie looked at him for a moment. I thought I saw white light flicker behind her shades, but I couldn't be sure.

"Anyway," I said. "Shall I see what I can see?"

"Umm, yes," Aunt Vanessa chirped. "Is there anything you need before you exorcise the ghost?"

I shook my head.

"It's not going to be an exorcism," I said. "Probably. I'll just find out where time's been damaged and smooth it over. They aren't the spirits of dead people. They're just broken bits of time clashing with each other."

Danny broke away from being stared at by Connie.

"Hang on," he said. "Can we do a couple of basic safety checks?"

Aunt Vanessa nodded. I sighed at the delay.

I put my hands in my pockets. A cold wind had started to cut through the aura of heat that nearly killing myself by riding a mountain bike had created.

Danny looked around the room, paying attention to the floor. Aunt Vanessa and whatever other archaeologists were on the scene had been digging around it. They'd got as far as revealing some old flagstones and the base of a chimney.

"Before you started digging, were there any fairy circles?" Danny asked.

Connie gave him a sharp look.

"I don't…" Aunt Vanessa said, shaking her head.

"He means circles of mushrooms," Connie said. "Which you wouldn't have found. Outside of cities you get them anywhere a lot of magic has been done – or anywhere there's fertile soil and plenty of water."

"Oh," Aunt Vanessa said. "Not inside."

A smile flicked across Danny's face.

"But you did get some outside?" he asked.

Aunt Vanessa nodded. She pointed out of the back window at a coppery, red-yellow circle of fungi that decorated the grass.

Connie sighed with irritation.

"That's not natural," she said. "Not outside a proper forest."

The archaeologists hadn't dug around the window, which meant the ground was still soft mud. It smacked and slopped, trying to cling to my shoes as I went up to the window. I reached out, trying to feel the age of the circle.

"How old is it?" Aunt Vanessa asked. "Does it go back to 1612?"

"Doesn't work like that," I said, trying to keep my senses in the past. "Time doesn't know we've divided it into minutes and hours. Time just is."

"Even if it was created by magic," Connie said. "That doesn't mean the people who lived here were sorcerers. At least, not the ones who were hanged as witches."

"Well, that's not quite true," Aunt Vanessa said. "There are records of people asking the family to cure their animals—"

"That doesn't mean they were doing magic," Connie snapped. "It just means they had some old recipes. Most of them were nonsense."

"Yeah," Danny said. "But what if they were sorcerers? We could be dealing with something dangerous—"

"Nobody's seen a revenant in two hundred years," Connie said. "They don't happen anymore."

"Can all three of you just take a deep breath please?" Aunt Vanessa asked, screwing her eyes closed. "What are you talking about?"

Connie looked pointedly at Danny, who made an 'after you' gesture. I kept my mouth shut. Connie looked back at him sourly, but started speaking.

"Some spirits do come back after death, usually magical people," Connie said. "They're intelligent, and they've got powerful magic. We call them revenants. I haven't seen one in two hundred years."

"Oh... if we had one, how much do you think it could tell us?" Vanessa asked.

"Nothing," Danny said. "Because you'd want to get rid of it."

"Oh yes, eventually, poor things, but they could tell us so much..." Vanessa said.

Danny frowned and shook his head.

"No way," Danny said. "It probably isn't a revenant, Connie's right about that, but if it is I'm going to take some pictures and then give it what it wants to get rid of it."

Connie crossed her arms again but looked slightly less angry than she had a minute ago. Aunt Vanessa frowned.

"What do you mean, 'give it what it wants?'" she asked.

"All revenants want something, that's why they come back," Connie said. "Unfortunately, sometimes they just want revenge on the living."

"Oh," Aunt Vanessa said. "Well, let's hope it doesn't want that."

We were getting back on territory I knew.

"Look," I asked. "Has it ever hit you or touched you? And has anyone ever had a proper two-way conversation with it?"

Aunt Vanessa looked relieved.

"Hostia, no, certainly not," she said. "It's just a little girl who asks the same few questions."

We all shared a look of relief.

"Doesn't sound like a revenant," Danny said, looking over at Connie.

"Aye," Connie said. "Let's hope not. Come on Fawkes, let's see it."

I felt around time, as carefully as I could. That's the trick with ghost hunting through time. If you're not careful, you can make new ones. I closed my eyes to get a better feel for the years as I pushed backwards.

Something moved.

"Hostia…" Aunt Vanessa said. "There she is."

There was a girl standing in the corner of the cottage. Her clothes were old and worn: a brown woollen dress and a linen apron. She was wearing a linen cap over uncombed hair and threadbare woollen shawl. She had shoes, but they weren't in a great condition.

She was painfully thin.

Connie and Danny had stepped between Aunt Vanessa and the little girl. I'll never forget the way she felt: time and space twisted so they didn't touch her.

"Danny…?" I asked.

Danny looked thoughtful and retied his dreads.

"I can draw a triangle around her if we want to talk."

"She's just a projection… hopefully…" Connie said.

"We could just try saying 'hello'," Danny said. "But she might try to rip off your face."

"Umm… is that still likely?" Aunt Vanessa asked.

Danny raised an eyebrow.

"Do you want to risk it?" he asked.

Connie rummaged in her bag and took out what looked like a snow globe filled with silvery goo.

"This is stupid. I'm going to talk to her. If she does anything, throw this," she said.

Aunt Vanessa took it gingerly, turning it over in her hands.

"Is this dangerous if you're not a ghost?" she asked.

Connie smirked.

"Only if you've got skin," she said.

Aunt Vanessa's eyes widened and she wrapped the globe in a hankie. Connie adjusted her shades and hunched down so she was level with the little girl. Anyone else would have taken the shades off, but in Connie's case that wouldn't have made her less threatening.

She pushed the shades up right against her face and gave the little girl a smile.

"Hello there," she said. "I'm Connie, what's your name?"

The little girl looked through her without answering.

"Would you like something to eat?" Connie asked, patting her pockets.

The little girl looked straight through her, fixed on something in the middle distance.

Connie took out a bag of nuts and raisins. She put a few of them in her hand, and then offered the bag.

"Do you want some of these? They're good."

The little looked at something next to her. She moved her lips silently, but it didn't look like she could see us.

"Have you got some chocolate?" Danny asked.

"She wouldn't know what it was," Connie said, shaking her head.

Aunt Vanessa made a thoughtful sound.

"So… would I be right in saying this proves she's definitely a ghost?" Vanessa asked.

Connie, Danny, and I looked at each other. The best answer we could come up with was 'hopefully.'

"Shall I touch her?" Connie asked.

"I wouldn't," Danny said.

Connie shook her head sadly.

"You're too young to be this cautious," Connie said.

Danny flashed her a smile.

"I've spent too much time with you," he said.

Connie edged towards the little girl. She touched her shoulder lightly.

"Nothing," Connie said. "Aunt V might be right. She's solid, though."

"That's okay," I said. "It could just be that the glitch in time is strong. I might be able to look back and see who she was?"

We all looked at each other. Nobody looked like they had any better ideas, and I was starting to feel silly about treating a half-starved little girl like an unexploded bomb.

I took a deep breath and reached back into the past; trying not to cause the same kind of damage I had in the field.

Something shifted nastily. Connie grabbed my shoulder. Danny was looking at me too.

"Fawkes… did you feel that?" Connie said.

"Is the little girl alright?" Aunt Vanessa asked.

The girl's eyes had turned jet black. She'd been pale, but now her skin was bone white. Her face looked like a thundercloud just before a storm. She looked at each of us in turn.

I let myself slip to my correct point in time, settling carefully into the present with as little disturbance as I could.

Her eyes settled on me. They weren't just black in colour; they were like holes in space.

"Witch," she said.

"Funny you should say that–" I said.

She lashed out with time magic. I can take myself back and forward, mostly. This was a huge, brutal shift. I tried to keep us in place and she just hit us harder.

"Mate?" Danny asked, stepping back.

He must have felt the second blow: time shifted underneath us, even Aunt Vanessa yelped as the sun flickered like a light switch.

"Throw the sphere," Connie said.

"Umm, are we sure it's the little girl?" Vanessa was pale.

"Just throw the ball," Connie shouted.

Vanessa's smile vanished.

"We can't know she's doing it," Vanessa said.

"She's the only black eyed monster kid I can see," Danny said. "She's a revenant. Throw the sphere."

The little girl's eyes flicked between us. I tried to get a better grip on holding us in the present.

"Do we have to kill her?" Vanessa asked.

Her face was a look of pure anguish. Danny looked back at her as if she'd gone mad.

"It's not going to kill her. Look at Esteban. He's not going to take another attack," Danny said.

Connie reached into her bag, burying her arm up to the elbow. Danny tried to grab the sphere off Aunt Vanessa, who instinctively tried to hold onto it.

The sphere dropped onto the floor, hitting a patch of recently dug flagstones. It shattered into fizzing white goo.

The little girl lashed out again. This force made me stagger; it was stronger than anything I'd ever felt. I screamed as she beat down my defences.

Time dissolved around us.

Chapter Four

Magic is a physical thing for me. For Danny it's all about maths and ideas. For Connie... I'm not sure. For me, it's like a part of my body. That's why I was blinded by pain as the little girl clubbed me with time magic.

The sky flickered through day and night so fast it looked like a strobe light. The seasons rushed past in a painful flash from hot to cold to hot again. I gasped for breath as the valley beyond was flooded and un-flooded again.

Finally, it was dark. The cottage was warm from the fire in the hearth, and dimly lit by a few stinking candles. They smelled like rancid pork fat. There was a low wooden ceiling above our heads now, which meant Danny and Connie had to stoop.

There was a woman. She was older than me, older than Aunt Vanessa was too. The little girl was standing in the corner, still looking at us with black eyes.

The woman spoke, not seeming to see us.

"Have you got any of that bread, our Jennet?" the woman asked.

Aunt Vanessa looked even more troubled than someone who had been dragged back through time by an angry magic-using ghost. She looked over to me and mouthed, 'that's not possible.'

The little girl ignored Aunt Vanessa and nodded to the older woman, offering a basket with a half-loaf of dry bread. Even with the shutters closed and the fire blazing, the cottage was still cold and draughty.

"This is power," Danny whispered.

Connie stepped closer, so that the four of us were huddled in one corner of the room.

"This is nothing," she whispered back. "Revenants can control the past in ways Esteban would never dream of."

A boy came in, shutting the cold night behind him. He looked about fourteen, with the same face and hair as the little girl. He had a dead lamb slung over his shoulder.

The little girl turned and looked at him. She spoke, but she looked more like she was play-acting than being part of the conversation.

"What's that?" she asked.

The boy looked at her uncertainly.

"It's a lamb," he said.

"I can see that, our James, where did ye get it?"

He shuffled back and hunched his shoulders. The little girl followed him, forcing him back towards the door.

"Did you take it?" she shouted.

He muttered something and looked at the older woman.

"We can't have this," Jennet said. "Not with our mam and gran–"

"Leave it be," the woman said. "We've got to eat something."

"Not that," Jennet said. "We can't eat that. We'll get in trouble."

"Not like we could get in any more trouble," said James.

Jennet turned on him. Her face was a mask of anger. Even if these people were just shadows in time, the memory was sweeping her away.

"Don't you ever think?" she said. "They'll be watching us."

"Calm down, pet," said the older woman.

"You're drunk," said Jennet. "My sister is going to hang, and you—"

The woman's eyes flashed with fury. She lashed out and gave the little girl a ringing slap around the face.

"You mind your tongue," she said. "Your granny said she'd sold her soul to the devil. It's a sin. A filthy bloody sin."

The woman broke off, shaking her head. She poured what smelled like beer from a leather bottle and took a long sip. She stared at her feet.

"My heart broke when your dad died," she said. "How do you think I felt when your mum said that it was Old Mrs. Chattox did it by witchcraft?"

"I'd never say a thing like that," the little girl said.

Her dark eyes teared up, but she didn't cry. She looked towards us again. The old woman looked at her bitterly.

"Don't be so daft. Of course you would. Everybody

would," she looked back at her feet.

"They said old Chattox's Tom took our mum's spinning wheel," the little girl said.

She looked towards us again. I glanced at Connie, who chewed her lip, then took a step forward.

"Aye. They're a bad lot," the older woman said.

Connie hunched down until she was level with the little girl.

"Is this what happened to your family?" she asked.

The little girl looked up at her, searching her face with those black eyes. I've got experience of creatures with weird eyes, but she still made me nervous. It wasn't because she was strange or different... there was just something wrong with the way she looked at us. Danny fished something out of his pocket and took a deep breath.

Conjuring isn't fast. Alchemists can prepare potions and jewels in advance, and I can do magic whenever I want, but if you want to have a magical battle with a conjurer they usually need six weeks warning and a room where they're allowed to draw on the floor.

Then again, Danny is quite creative.

"Do you think I can bind a revenant, mate?" Danny asked, whispering.

"I don't know."

The old woman passed a blunt, thick bladed knife to the boy.

"You'd best get started with that," she said. "The others'll be coming soon."

Jennet looked away from Connie.

"We can't be doing this," the girl said.

"It's Good Friday," the older woman answered, taking another sip of her beer. "We'll celebrate the day with our friends and our kin; remind them all we're good Christians."

"It's not a lot, Mam," the boy said.

"You're all right, our Jimmy," the woman said. "You did well."

Connie touched the girl on the shoulder; she spun around, her black eyes wide. I couldn't tell if she was angry or surprised, but she brushed Connie's hand off and took a step back.

"Please," Connie asked. "What are you trying to tell us? Is this what happened to you? What year was it?"

"What would you say, if they took you?" The little girl asked.

Aunt Vanessa sighed. She watched the little girl with open pity. I'm good with magic, but I don't spend much time around people. It's hard to stay in school when you can accidentally drift back and forwards in time. I watched Connie and I wished I had a clue if she was doing the right thing.

"They did take me, a long time ago," Connie said. "But I was lucky, and a friend got me out of it."

The little girl frowned for a second, and then looked at Danny.

"What about you? What would you say if they took you?" she asked.

Danny shrugged.

"I don't know," he said. "I don't think anyone knows

until it happens."

She didn't seem to care about Aunt Vanessa, or maybe she could tell Aunt Vanessa wasn't a magical person. The little girl looked past her to me. I thought about Abuela and what she'd do if she were ever captured by witch hunters.

It made me feel sorry for them, to be honest.

"What would you do? Would you tell them what they wanted?" the little girl asked.

I'm short. I'm fat. I can't run or do anything physical. I'm not cool, I only have two friends, and people say my grandmother makes me act old. All I am is stubborn and unlucky with a magical gift that even other sorcerers think is weird. It's why I said what I said next.

She looked up at me and asked again: "Would you tell them what they wanted?"

I thought about it for a second.

"No," I said. "I wouldn't."

The others looked like I'd just kicked a beehive. The little girl's black eyes fixed on me. Her face twisted with anger. She balled her fists up so tightly they were white.

"Everybody talks," she said. "Everybody tells."

She grabbed a handful of time. I could feel her going for another big shift. From the way she was dragging me back with her, she knew it hurt and didn't care.

"Danny?" I asked. "If you've got anything you can do, this is the time."

Danny's tall. I'm taller than the little girl is, and

Danny towers over me. He took a slim black wand out of his pocket and held it over the little girl's head.

"Oh, wicked spirit that obeyeth me not," his voice echoed, infused with magical power. "I enclose and bind you in this triangle of art—"

Danny pressed a stud on the wand and a triangle of light glowed into life.

"Is that magic?" Aunt Vanessa whispered.

I didn't answer. I closed my eyes and tried hold back against the little girl's magic. Connie looked back to Aunt Vanessa and whispered.

"No," She said. "I think he modified a laser pointer."

It might have worked. The little girl looked up in shock and I did feel some power crackling through the triangle.

The problem with shapes made out of light is they're easy to break. Something – a moth, a fly, or just a bit of ash from the fire – broke the beam.

The triangle collapsed. Magical energy disappeared.

The little girl ripped time out from under us.

Chapter Five

Time changed around us. The light changed – night turned into a cold spring day – and it was raining. Everything was wet. The straw on the floor stank of rot and my clothes stank of damp. A chill cut straight through into my bones.

The door rattled on its hinges as someone pounded it hard. The only thing holding it shut was a wooden bar, which didn't look like it would hold against much of an assault.

"We're still in the cottage?" Aunt Vanessa asked.

"Yeah," said Danny. "It feels warmer, though."

"Dan?" I asked. "If you've got a new friend to invoke, this might be the time."

Danny shook his head.

"No way," he said. "We're not in that much trouble."

I looked at him like he'd lost his mind. The door rattled with another flurry of knocking. It made a nasty crack as the force split the wood.

The older woman from before came scurrying from upstairs.

"Hold on, hold on," she said, jogging down the steps. "I'll be with ye."

"Mum!" It was the voice of the boy who'd stolen the lamb. "Muuuuuuum."

The woman ran straight past us to the door.

"Our James, what the devil is wrong?" she asked.

She'd barely drawn the bar away when the door burst inward. James, the boy we'd seen a moment ago, squirmed between a pair of burly men in work clothes.

"Elizabeth Device?" another man asked, stepping forward.

He looked better off than the other two, but just as strong. He looked like he'd worked in the fields in his time, or maybe something that involved many knives, since he had thick scars on his hands. He had blue eyes and thick black beard.

"You know who I am, Henry Hargreaves," the older woman, Elizabeth, said. "You know me of old."

Hargreaves looked at her.

"That I do," he said. "Your boy took a lamb from the field."

Elizabeth met his gaze with steel.

"Aye," she said, raising her chin. "What if he did? We have to have something to eat if God won't provide for us."

Hargreaves shuffled his feet. For a minute, I thought he was going to take a step backwards, but he didn't. His hand hovered over his chest, like he wanted to cross himself, but he didn't do that, either.

"We've had reports that you're doing things you shouldn't be," Hargreaves said, looking away.

Elizabeth Device glowered at him fiercely.

"We've been doing nothing but the good Christian celebration of Easter and the Sabbath," she said.

Hargreaves looked back at her.

"Sabbat did you say?" he leaned until they stood

nose to nose.

"Watch what you say, Henry Hargreaves," Elizabeth said. "If there are witches here, you should have a care for angering me."

I looked over at the others.

"I don't like the way this is going..." I said.

The little girl opened her eyes, they were deep and black as night. Even looking at her gave me a sickly pain in the back of my head. It was like space and time did what she said to avoid touching her.

She gave me a filthy look.

"Hey," I said, waving my hands between us. "Look, I'm sorry; I didn't mean to say anything stupid. Danny's right, I don't know anything without it happening to me. You're right–"

I felt a wave of power come off her. Something changed. It felt like a joint slipping out of the socket, only more weird than painful.

That was when one of men holding James Device pointed straight at us with a look of horror on his face.

"Sweet God, what are they?"

Chapter Six

Everything after that happened really quickly.

It turned out there were six of them plus Henry Hargreaves, who grabbed hold of James Device.

James and his mother cried out in fright, not used to seeing people in strange clothes appear in their living room without warning. Two burly farmers each went after Danny and me, more interested in grabbing us than hurting us.

Danny shoved me out of the way of one and then ducked under another. Three others joined in – I didn't look like I needed three people to capture me, to be honest. They chased Danny out of the open window.

The one who was after me grinned and lunged at me, except I wasn't there.

The little girl didn't want me to move through time. Every second I could feel her trying to hold me in place, but I didn't need to move far. As he reached for me, I stopped and vanished, appearing near the opposite window to the one from which Danny had escaped. The effort gave me spots in front of my eyes.

The other two went for Connie and Aunt Vanessa, which they regretted. Archaeology might not be quite as action packed as in the films, but Aunty V still packed a punch. He stepped forward and she socked him straight in the mouth, sending him staggering back with a look of shock on his face.

The funny thing was the other one. First, he made towards Connie, who backed away, rummaging through her things. If I'd have been paying better attention, I would have felt sorry for him. I've seen the sorts of things that can come out of Connie's bag.

He was a big man. He advanced on her, as if she was a horse that might kick him in the face. Connie backed away, giving ground without backing herself into a corner. She stepped out of the way to avoid walking into the girl - Jennet. Personally, I was ready to dangle the kid by the ankles for putting us in so much trouble, but Connie's a better person than I am. Also, Connie whipped a glass tube out of her bag and poured it all over her.

The man's eyes bulged. He looked between them.

"You…" he said.

A beautiful look of horror crossed Jennet's face as she realized he could see her. She tried to dart away, but he grabbed her wrist.

He held her off the ground, her feet kicking. I'd have left her there, but as I said, Connie's a better person than I am.

"Oi!" Connie yelled, stepping up to the big man, giving him a sharp kick in the ankle. "How do you like that?"

I don't know if Connie went off to a monastery and trained in some lost, shin-kicking martial art, or if it was just a lucky kick, but a man twice her size screamed in pain and fell.

That was the moment when Elizabeth Device raised

her voice and bellowed over the chaos.

"STOP!" she shouted. "I WILL NOT HAVE THIS FIGHTING IN MY HOUSE."

Jennet looked around, taking a step back into the corner. Just for a second, her grip loosened and I thought I might be able to take us back to the present, but she clamped down hard.

"What's wrong, is this not the way it happened?" I asked her, taking my chance to side step towards the window. "This is the danger when you mess with time, even with your power."

She looked back at me with cold black eyes.

"I couldn't make it worse if I tried," she replied.

The man who'd been facing down Aunt Vanessa stepped back, guarding against another punch.

"Aye," he said. "Ye've got nothing to fear if you've done nothing wrong."

"I've heard that before," I muttered.

"You're the one who appeared out of thin air," said the man who'd been chasing me.

I tried to think of an excuse that wouldn't get me burned as a witch or locked up as a mad person. Nothing popped into my head.

"I won't let you hurt them," said Connie.

Hargreaves sighed and pinched the bridge of his nose.

"I don't want to hurt anyone," he said. "I'm an officer of the court and I want to investigate this case."

"They appeared out of thin air," insisted the man.

Hargreaves looked into the house and shrugged.

"It's bright out here and dark in there. I could have missed them at first, I don't know about you," he said.

The man shrugged unwillingly.

"They've got a black-a-moor boy. They say the Devil appears as a black-a-moor," he said.

Hargreaves cut him off with a stern look.

"Oh, shut up. There's men from Afrik and Ethiop who weren't nothing worse than you or I," Hargreaves said. "And I've known Englishmen who were the Devil himself."

Elizabeth Device, who'd been standing quietly and shaking, looked at Hargreaves. Her face was red, savage from anger and fear.

"These are no devils of mine, Henry Hargreaves," she said. "I won't have it said I had devils in my house."

"Aye," said Hargreaves. "If they come quietly, we just want to ask this lad a few questions."

He nodded at James, who looked pleadingly at his mother. She looked at Jennet, who stood silently between Connie and me. The waves of power coming off her made me feel ill. Hargreaves stooped down to Jennet's level.

"We might have a few questions for this lovely young lady as well," he said, flashing a smile full of rotten teeth.

The girl looked back at him with expressionless, black-eyed malice.

I couldn't hear Danny or the other three men outside, unless he'd given up quietly. It was possible; Conjurers don't have much they can do in the short term. If you lock one in a room with a piece of chalk, though, they can make a lot of trouble.

Hargreaves looked.

"Which will it be? Quiet or loud? I can find another twenty bailiffs, I dare say, if I have the need to," Hargreaves said.

Connie shook her head unwillingly, but stepped away from Jennet, who barely reacted. Aunt Vanessa dropped her fists to her sides and nodded.

"I think that's your answer," I said.

Hargreaves nodded once, and the bailiffs grabbed each one of us by the shoulder. White light flickered behind Connie's shades, which was as close as she came to being able to glare. The bailiff looked surprised, but didn't say anything else.

"You're going to burn," the man whispered.

"Only if you take me to Scotland," Connie said, loud enough for me to hear. "We haven't burned a witch in England for centuries."

"Alright, outside," Hargreaves said. "We have something to ask of the young man."

Elizabeth Device glared at us, but the look she gave Hargreaves was of total disgust. She looked from her son to the parish constable and back.

"I know you of old, Henry Hargreaves," she said. "I thought better of ye."

Hargreaves glanced at her, and pushed James harder than he needed. The boy walked nervously out into the yard, leading the way to a patch in the tiny herb garden.

I walked next to Jennet. The girl was too small for the bailiff to lead her by the shoulder, so he'd decided to tow her by the hand. She followed him, looking straight ahead with the same look of blank malice she'd had from the beginning.

"I don't know what you're getting out of this," I said. "But you've got to stop. We'll help you get what you want…"

"Oi," said the bailiff leading me. "No talking."

The little girl didn't turn to look at me; she just looked straight ahead and spoke, like she was talking to the whole world.

"Everybody tells," she said. "That's the rule: everybody tells and everybody lies."

"Enough of that," our bailiffs snapped.

James led the way with Hargreaves, but it was agonizing to watch. He took a few steps, then looked back at the parish constable, who indicated by pointing his head. He wandered a few steps more, and stopped again. This time Hargreaves hardly moved his head at all, and James turned pale, darting around the back of the house between a dung heap and a pile of stones.

He stopped again and looked at the constable, confused.

"Is this the patch you told me about?" he asked. "Between the stones and the midden, right down there by the wall?"

"Let's all clap for the justice of the past, shall we?" Connie said, smiling bitterly.

"You mind your tongue," her bailiff said, shifting his

feet. "She's a witch and ye're all witches."

"Do what you like," Connie said. "This disgusts me."

"Maybe the witch needs to be scratched," said another bailiff.

"That's enough of you," Hargreaves said. "If there's anything wrong with what I'm doing, it'll be a matter for the Judge."

I looked at Hargreaves.

"Why are you bothering? You can do anything you want." I said.

Hargreaves' face flushed. He turned back to James Device.

"Is this the place, boy?" Hargreaves asked, his voice rough with anger.

The boy nodded. The black-eyed girl watched expressionlessly, looking at us, and then at a patch of freshly turned earth.

"Oh come on," I said. "You buried that five minutes ago."

"You mind your tongue," one of the bailiffs snarled.

"Or what?" I asked. "You didn't do well last time."

Hargreaves let a hand drop to the wooden club on his belt.

"If you try our patience again," he said. "We might forget that we're men of compassion."

It was quite a big club.

"Oh," I said.

Hargreaves coughed. He clapped a hand on James Device's shoulder.

"If I should dig there, what do you think I should find?" he asked.

James looked at his mother and sister, and then looked at us, but with more confusion on his face. The little girl stared straight ahead with a look of intense concentration.

I could feel the little girl's grip on time loosening. Even she didn't have the power to keep this going forever. I took a deep breath and got ready to try another move to the present.

Connie must have noticed too. She shoved the little girl in the shoulder.

"I hope you enjoy what happens next," she said. "Because you're about to live it all over again. Are you looking forward to that?"

Hargreaves unhooked the cudgel off his belt and brandished it.

"Quiet. Who wants it first?" he said, growling through his teeth.

"She started it," Connie said, pointing at the little girl.

"I'll tell that to the magistrate," Hargreaves said. "Now silence from all of ye, or I might decide you need swimming."

"He doesn't mean a trip down to the Leisure Centre, does he?" I whispered.

Connie replied with a silent shake of her head. Aunt Vanessa had given up smiling and stared straight ahead, wringing her hands. I'd never before seen anyone literally wring his or her hands with worry.

Then again, I've never been in a situation like this before. My grandmother would have owned it…which is something I wasn't doing. Time solidified around me. I had to stop talking to Hargreaves and concentrate on the magic. I could feel the little girl's grip on time trembling, but she was still stronger than I was.

Hargreaves turned back to James Device.

"If I dig here," he asked. "What will I find?"

James looked at him uncomprehendingly for a moment, until Hargreaves' face darkened with rage. He opened his mouth, stunned by the effort of remembering what he'd been told to say.

"I… our Grandma buried a picture here, full of pins," he said.

James looked at Hargreaves hopefully. The parish constable patted him roughly on the shoulder.

"Aye," he said. "There's a good lad. Dig."

James looked at him uncomprehendingly again for a minute, then knelt down and started uncovering the earth with his hands. I tried to resist the urge to lean closer and look at what was being uncovered.

Aunt Vanessa shook her head.

"We have to get away from this," she whispered.

"I know," I said.

My aunt fidgeted and twitched.

"Please, what if they take us away and put us in a cellar that isn't there anymore? What if we get hanged for witchcraft?" she said.

I closed my eyes and tried to block out her words. I could feel the little girl's attention weakening. Any second now, I'd get my chance.

The little girl wasn't looking straight ahead anymore, she was watching, leaning closer and closer to see her brother digging in the earth.

"Here it is," James said. "Our granny buried it."

"Oh good god," Aunt Vanessa said.

It was a wax doll. Even filthy from being buried in the earth, I could see there were bits of hair and fingernails buried in it. It was stuck through with rusty metal pins.

"They didn't make that, you did," I said, losing my concentration again.

"No he didn't," Aunt Vanessa said, staring at the doll. "It's been in the earth for weeks. And look at the pins. They're cheap drawn wire, just the sort you'd get from a roadside pedlar."

"What?" I looked between Connie and my aunt.

Connie shook her head.

"I-I don't know... some people who were burned as witches might have been doing magic. It doesn't mean they were magical people. Bloodied Nails..."

Aunt Vanessa looked to the little girl, her fear forgotten.

"Is this what you wanted to show us?" she asked.

The little girl looked back at Vanessa. Her eyes and skin didn't change, but she looked ordinary, frightened and human. Her lips quivered as she tried to find the right shape for what she wanted to say.

That was when Danny came back.

Chapter Seven

A huge, angry man-bird exploded the bubble of trapped time.

We all felt it coming, and Connie and I knew exactly what it was. We've previously done heavy magic with Medimiel. He looks like a cute, clueless birdman, but he's an Angel.

You can read a lot about when Angels get angry. There's a book called Paradise Lost.

Danny shouldn't have been able to put something together this quickly. Conjurers need hours – sometimes weeks – to make their magic work. It's one of the reasons they like to make friends with Chronomancers: you can do a lot more when you have a friend who can literally stop time.

Don't make any mistake though, when they get going, conjurers can do impressive things. Between Connie, Danny and me, we stopped a demon stealing the City of London. I've seen Medimiel face down a huge fire spirit and come away even.

Medimiel's anger throbbed in our bones. If you can't imagine that, count yourselves lucky. Connie must have felt it at the same time I did. She looked into the distance, looked at me, and hit the deck.

I did the same thing, covering my head. By now, the grass was vibrating from the force of the magical energy.

Hargreaves, the bailiffs and the Device family stopped. I don't mean they stood still or just stopped talking. They stopped like a dodgy DVD. Hargreaves flickered in and out of existence. James Device stood, looking at the hole in the ground. Elizabeth Device was trapped in the same puzzled head movement, glitching over and over again.

The only one who wasn't affected was Jennet. Her eyes were wide and black, her mouth a little 'o' of panic.

Aunt Vanessa looked over to me.

"What's going on?" she asked.

"It's Danny," I shouted. "He's breaking through."

I was shouting this because my magical senses had decided – too late – to announce that something magical was about to put me in danger. Some Chronomancers see a white rabbit. Others see flashing lights or get a pain in their joints. I hear a weird, tooth-jarring tune that I call 'The Devil's Ringtone.'

The little girl's eyes narrowed. I felt her throw a huge amount of power against the oncoming force. The air turned purple. A nasty, tinny, greasy taste forced its way into my mouth.

"Oh god," said my Aunt, who couldn't sense the oncoming storm. "Is there anything I should do?"

Connie looked up from where she was lying face down with her head covered.

"Can you see what I'm doing?" she asked.

The clash of power was huge now, but I still couldn't see Danny. Blue and purple light flickered around the edges of Malkin Tower. If we'd have been in the city we would have been able to see buildings flickering in and out of existence, but some moorland in the 17th century looks pretty much the same four hundred years later.

My hair started to stand on end.

That was something Aunt Vanessa could see.

"Hostia…" she said, staring at me and Connie's hair floating on an unfelt breeze.

Then she dived for something, tackling it out of Hargreaves' semi-transparent hand, and curled up on the ground.

The little girl hissed like a cat.

I wish I could say I turned things around but I was just the straw that broke the camel's back. Once Aunt Vanessa was safe, I reached out and gave as big a shove with time-magic as I could.

The little girl screamed a shrill, cut-off, human scream and vanished. The house and everything in it burst into cold blue flame and burned away. Four hundred years rushed past, with each one kicking me in the stomach as it went.

Finally, the real world lurched into position.

I lay in the mud, my head pounding. I stayed down and kept my eyes closed. The last time we went through a magical event this big I opened the door to find half the Metropolitan Police.

"Is everyone okay? Connie? Auntie V? Jennet?" I asked.

"Jennet's gone," Danny said. "I'm alright too, by the

way."

"That's a surprise," I said. "What happened to her?"

Danny sighed.

"I didn't see much, she just popped out of existence."

Danny helped me to my feet. He was shaking his head but he was smiling. I realized it was alright.

"How long have we been gone?" I asked, helping Aunt Vanessa.

"It's about two in the morning," Danny said. "So… maybe about fifteen hours?"

"No wonder I feel so weak," Aunt Vanessa said, peering into the darkness. "Can anyone see where I left the bikes?"

"Can't we go back to the Land Rover?" I asked. "I feel like I've been hit by a rugby team."

"I'd rather not," she said. "I know the way back to the cottage from here, but I don't fancy driving around country roads at this time of night."

If it hadn't been so dark, she would have been able to see the look I gave her.

"This means another hour of cycling, doesn't it?" I asked.

"Cheer up," Aunt Vanessa said. "It's getting you fit."

The next half-hour was a hell of nervousness and exhaustion as we cycled through country lanes and every maniac in Lancashire drove with their foot clamped down on the accelerator. Cars whooshed past, honking their horns as they screeched around corners. At one point even Danny lost his balance and had to jump onto the embankment (for him, it's big deal... for me, it means we reached a turning).

"They're idiots on the roads at night here," Vanessa said. "Welcome home, though."

We turned off the road into the front yard of a farmhouse. A horseshoe of buildings surrounded the square flagstone yard. It was quite cool when Aunt Vanessa activated the floodlights with her key ring. Everything was new and scrubbed.

"It's incredibly modern inside," Aunt Vanessa said. "It's a guest house normally, but my friend Dorothy let me borrow it."

After the accursed bikes were locked up in a barn that was now a warm room full of exercise equipment we stumbled into the kitchen. It was all pine and ceramic tiles.

It was also incredibly clean. Too clean.

"Have we got any food?" I asked, looking.

"Ah..." Aunt Vanessa said.

"I brought a load of stuff in my bags," I said. "But all of that is gone."

Connie gave me a look of genuine horror.

"All that Parma ham and chorizo?" she asked.

"Gone," I said.

Danny laughed and shook his head.

"You two are brilliant," he said, smiling. "Is there anything at all?"

"I don't really cook for myself much, it's a bit of a faff for one," Aunt Vanessa said, then brightened. "Still, if we hop on the bikes we could cycle down to the twenty-four hour shop in the village."

I couldn't have been more worried if the little girl had appeared.

"I'll die," I said. "I'll die, and I'll use the last of my strength to text Abuela."

"You stay here and make tea," Danny said, picking his helmet up again. "Night cycling's awesome, I'll come."

Aunt Vanessa gave him a beam of approval.

"Good man," she said, and turned to Connie. "Can we tempt you?"

Connie yawned and almost took off her shades. If I hadn't semi-gasped, she probably would have, without thinking.

"Umm, no," Connie said, pushing her shades back. "I've never been so tired."

Aunt Vanessa rolled her eyes and then yawned.

"Hmm," Vanessa shook herself awake. "Well, maybe I'm a bit shattered too, but someone's got to get you lot fed."

She stood up and gave Danny another approving smile.

"Come on," she grinned. "Work party, fall in."

Once they'd unchained the bikes and their lights had vanished down the lane, Connie took off her shades.

It takes a lot of magic to live over three hundred and fifty years. For Connie, the price had been her eyes: under her shades, she just had two hollow, glowing holes in her face.

"Sorry," she said, rubbing her face. "I can't wear

those a minute longer."

"That's okay," I said, prodding her in the arm. "Are you okay?"

"It's strange to find sorcerers and Cunning Folk on trial for witchcraft," Connie said. "My father tried a few witches, and he always said they weren't magical people."

I'd never heard the word 'Cunning Folk'. Connie must have seen the question in my face.

"They mostly helped people," she explained. "Sometimes they were magical people, other times they just knew a bit of medicine and herb lore. They were useful, to be honest. I used to get most of my medicines from Mother Lovelock in Islington."

"Shall I make some tea?" I asked.

"Only if there isn't any Coke," Connie said.

There wasn't, so Connie had to settle for a cup of tea with five sugars. I also turned on every light I could find. After the stuff at Malkin Tower, the farmhouse didn't feel safe: the walls felt thin and papery, as if anything could walk through them at any minute.

"That was weird," I said. "Back at the cottage."

"Indeed... you know, I can't believe I'm going to sleep here," Connie said.

"What do you mean?"

"It's magically neutral," Connie said, the torchlight-glow of her gaze following the bottoms of the walls. "No protection."

"Oh," I said.

"Do you suppose that little girl's spirit has gone?"

Connie asked.

I'd just started thinking the same thing. I finished making my cup of tea with a sudden knot of worry in my chest.

"We could make a temporary wall with some salt," Connie said. "If we can find any."

I was about to start searching the cupboards when I felt something cold, like a breeze, blast through the brick walls. The Devil's Ringtone chimed once.

Something cold and wet touched my hand.

I yelped and pulled back, jumping so much that I nearly fell out of my seat. A slightly hurt looking spaniel looked back at me.

There was something wrong with it. I couldn't tell you what: it looked like a cute dog... but there was no way it could have gotten in the kitchen. The doors were still fastened and the back door was closed via the deadlock.

The dog nudged my hand with its head and I stroked it, looking for any signs of a secret dog flap it could have used.

I looked into the pools of light that passed for Connie's eyes. She didn't look much happier than I was.

It had the same feel as Jennet. Whatever it was, I couldn't tell you... but it didn't feel like it should have been there.

Connie looked back at me, and looked at the dog. It shivered as the light from her eyes fell on its fur.

I touched the dog's head. It moved silently, pressing

into my hand. I felt stomach-churningly nervous and stupid at the same time.

"Could it be the farm dog...?" I suggested. "I mean, we might be just being paranoid."

"Look at that," Connie said, and nodded at something in the corner.

Our bags, everything that had been lost in the place between worlds, stood in the corner of the kitchen.

I looked down at the dog.

"Was that you?" I asked, ruffling the dog's fur. "Are you Danny's new friend?"

I was still using the sort of tone you'd usually use if you were talking to a dog. If I stopped pretending it was a dog, then it might reveal itself as whatever it really was.

I wasn't sure I was ready for that.

"Was that you, boy?" I asked again, scratching in the dog's head.

It looked back at me silently. Its eyes were the wrong thing, I realized. They were too big, and too old. I'd never seen eyes like that on an animal.

"Right... just to test if you understand me," I said, still feeling both nervous and stupid. "One bark for yes, two for no."

The dog stopped wagging its tail, looked at me seriously, and spoke in plain English.

"I did that," the dog said. "And I could do more."

It didn't sound like a dog. There was nothing doggy or animal about its speech. It looked at me, opened its mouth, and out came words.

"What's your name?" I asked, in a more normal tone.

The dog-thing backed away. You might think finding a talking dog would be cool. At the time, it was slightly terrifying.

"You can call me Tom," the dog said. "And I could do much for you."

"What kind of 'much'?" I asked.

I glanced sideways at Connie, who got up silently and put on her dark glasses. The dog didn't seem to care about her. It went on looking straight at me.

"Money, power," it said. "You'd never go hungry; never have to take orders from anyone again."

"Right..." I said. "This is sudden..."

"You have potential," said the dog, which was really freaking me out by now. "I can see that."

"I think Danny's probably got more–" I started saying.

"He is nothing," the dog snapped. "You have the potential, with my help."

Connie had left the table completely and was industriously searching through various kitchen drawers. I tried to catch her eye without visibly looking at her, which meant I looked sideways at her again for a moment.

"I don't think I'm up for it, being honest," I said.

I would have got up and walked away. I wanted to put space between the dog and myself. Unfortunately, I couldn't move a muscle. I just sat and stared at the dog, not even able to look away.

"Follow me and you'll never have to fear the dark again," the dog said. "Or the spirits that walk there."

"No," I said.

It was like speaking through treacle. I didn't feel like it was trying to force me to say yes, but it didn't want to make it easy for me to say no.

"Anyway, I don't believe you'd do it for free," I said. "And I don't want to pay."

"It wouldn't be anything you'd miss," the dog said. "Or anything you're using."

I just wanted to say no and get up, but I couldn't. Even speaking felt like too much, it was like the air had increased in weight, pressing down on me. All I could do was stare at the dog in a disapproving manner and hope it went away.

The animal cocked its head.

"Getting hard to breath?" it asked.

It hadn't been, but once the dog said so my chest muscles burned with effort.

My brain fluttered. I reached out with time magic, but the creature didn't seem to exist in time. I'd never seen that with either an angel or a demon.

I took in another lead-weight breath. How many more would I manage?

"One word and it goes away," the dog said.

I tried to shake my head, but I couldn't even manage that. I shifted back and forth in time, but the dog followed me, still sitting there no matter where I went. I snapped back to the present.

I tried to take another breath, but it was too hard.

The air whistled out of my lungs as I breathed out helplessly. A dim red haze seemed to fill the room. I wanted to get up and run around, yelling in panic. The dog just sat and stared.

"One word," it said.

I wanted to yell out for Connie. My panicked brain screamed at her, but I couldn't make a sound.

That was when Connie threw salt over us both, intoning in the language of magic.

"OEL AMMEMA ILS," her voice boomed and echoed more than it should have. "OEL AMMEMA ILS, IN CORAXO QUASABEH. GAHA ERMES ODEH GAHA GABRIEL, COMO COMSELHA."

The dog boiled into blue fire and vanished.

I still couldn't move or breathe much.

"What was that?" I asked, gasping for air.

Connie shook her head curtly and went to the edge of the room. She'd found a huge tub of salt in one of the cupboards, and she used it to mark a circle of salt around the dinner table and us.

As the salt circle closed, I felt something snap. I took a whooping breath as my body worked again.

"Hostia..." I sat, breathing a lungful of salty air. "Seriously, what was that?"

Connie pointed out of the window.

"I'm not the one you should be asking," she said.

I looked out into the darkness. The floodlights were still on, lighting a single pale figure, standing in the courtyard. Jennet Device stood in the floodlights, her black eyes shining.

Chapter Eight

We moved the table so that Connie could sit on floor and keep up the magical defences. A barrier of salt isn't the best thing against a magical attack but it's a lot better than nothing. After an hour, I managed to find a marker pen and drew some of the usual characters of magic around the edge, just inside Connie's wobbly border of salt. It was more a 'slightly mystical oblong' than a magical circle, but it Jennet couldn't get through it. Yet.

It was getting light. Sunlight makes it harder to do magic, but not as hard as it makes things for spirits. By half past six, the little girl was much weaker. Barely the strongest magical force we'd ever felt. Her blows against the barrier were only slightly stronger than a speeding truck.

"In Gaha Gabriel Odeh G-Gaha Raphael," Connie said, stumbling over the words.

My hastily marked magical words were fading as fast as I was trying to redraw them. Danny would have done better, but Danny's a trained Conjurer.

The little girl was still standing there, in the yard, clear in the daylight. Her coal black eyes shone in the light. Her face looked more alien when you could see how huge her eyes were.

That was when I heard my Aunt Vanessa's voice.

"...should be back in time for everyone to have a fried breakfast and then get some sleep," she said. "We can talk about what happened later–"

She stopped talking, as she saw the little girl standing in the courtyard.

There was a moment's silence, and then Danny spoke.

"Are you alright in there, guys?" he asked.

I risked reaching over to open the window a crack, and shouted back to him.

"Yeah, we're alright," I shouted. "Do you want to go back and get some cakes?"

Danny grinned, but I could see the recognition in his eyes. On the floor behind me, Connie was stuttering and stumbling over her words. The little girl was pushing, and pushing and pushing, but Connie was alive and more or less human. Her invocation had dwindled a murmur, heavy with tiredness.

Connie's spell broke. The door swung open languidly, letting in a shaft of early morning sunlight.

Connie's eyes closed completely and she slumped in on herself. If she hadn't already been sitting on the floor she would have collapsed. The light that usually shone out behind her eyelids was dim. Her hands dropped to her sides.

The magical barrier dissolved. Without Connie to shore it up the salt wasn't strong enough to hold out, and I don't know what I'm doing. Danny looked on and shouted something.

Henry Hargreaves, the local bailiff, formed out of shadow and weak sunlight. Other figures, more than ten, formed behind him holding sticks and improvised weapons.

He reached down and took Jennet's hand, leading her forward.

"I was told I'd find you here," he said, looking at my marks on the floor. "I daresay you'll make your attempt at disappearing again."

"Jennet," I said. "I don't know why you showed me that dog, but I can help you find what you're looking for. We have a great Conjurer and an Alchemist. Aunt Vanessa can find out anything you need—"

"I showed you nothing," Jennet said.

She looked up at Hargreaves.

"I saw them flying over church," she piped. "And one of them told my mother that he killed Redfearne's cow."

"Aye," said Hargreaves. "I believe you."

Hargreaves stepped over the line of salt. It had enough power to make him hesitate for a split second.

I grabbed time and held it tight, stopping it dead. The little girl reacted, but too late. I could feel her pushing against me, but this time I had the upper hand.

I grabbed Connie under the arms and shook her.

"Connie? Connie!" I said, and tried to drag her to her feet. "We need to move."

Connie shook her head and struggled against me weakly.

"Connie!" I shouted. Then I grabbed her ear and

twisted it.

Her eyes flew open.

"Ow, Blooded Nails, what are you–?" she said, taking in the situation. "Oh."

Connie saw Hargreaves at the door and snatched up her bag, scrambling to her feet.

Time started moving again.

We ran through the dining room into the living room. Unfortunately, we'd only protected the kitchen. Six men with cudgels rushed towards us.

Behind us, in the kitchen, the little girl spoke in a shrill voice.

"There they are," she said. "They're in the parlour."

The six men advanced on us. I'm not very good at fighting, especially not when they're better armed and twice my size. I dodged a blow from a cudgel and backed towards the door, where I could hear more bailiffs coming through and forcing the doors that led to the barn and the outhouses.

"In the parlour," Hargreaves called, following just behind us. "This way."

The stairs, trendy and modern without a banister or anything on the side, stuck out of the wall next to us. I stepped towards them. One of the men darted forwards and grabbed my ankle.

A glass tube smashed on his tunic. He burst into a shower of magic.

"Go!" shouted Connie, juggling a handful of tubes and bottles from her bag.

The bailiffs roared and I ran up the stairs. My legs

already felt like raw meat, after spending the day on the bikes. It's surprising what you can do when you're in danger of being arrested by witch hunters from the past, though. I powered to the top with more breath than I expected and looked around for the next flight. Connie bolted up the stairs after me.

"Up!" she shouted, pointing at the next flight of stairs.

She ran holding her shades to her face with one hand. She threw a glass vial at the next bailiff to the top of the stairs. This time blue fire burst out from the smashed bottle and banished him into the past.

The next floor up was just more bedrooms. A distracted part of me noticed that the bathrooms here were nice. Connie was coming up the stairs behind me, jogging backwards so she didn't have to turn away from the bailiffs still chasing us.

I wondered if there was a fire escape on the outside of the building. I decided not to think about it too much.

One of the bailiffs threw his cudgel and it hit Connie on the side of the face. She cried out in pain, and threw another bottle of alchemical tincture back at him. This one broke and turned him into gold. He burst into a shower of magical energy and vanished.

"Are you alright?" I asked.

The side of her face was red, and already starting to swell.

"Just go!" she said.

Behind us, we could hear the little girl shouting accusations from the living room. Apparently, she didn't want to follow us up the stairs.

"How many of those things have you got?" I asked, backing up the next flight of stairs. There was no way the farmhouse was more than three floors.

"Another four," Connie said. "I didn't think I'd need them for this."

"Can you mix more?" I asked.

We'd reached the top. I looked around, trying to work out which direction gave us the most space to run. Peach and white landings stretched off in two directions, lined with sturdy-looking doors.

"This way," Connie said, and pointed. "I think it goes back over the barn."

"Nice one," I said, and started running.

"Hang on," Connie said.

There was a wardrobe standing at the top of the stairs. Connie shoved a glass bottle behind it and gave it a kick. A muffled explosion hurled the wardrobe down until it wedged in the stairway. By the sound of it, she managed to squash a couple more bailiffs.

"How many bailiffs did you count?" I asked, jogging down the corridor.

"Who knows?" Connie said. "For all I know she's pulling them straight back from the past as I banish them."

All the bedrooms were open and empty, which was one good thing. Although, having a couple of confused tourists between the bailiffs and us could have bought us time.

We ran through a bedroom into an en-suite

bathroom... and a wall.

Behind us, it sounded as if the bailiffs were breaking through the wardrobe.

"They don't make them like they used to," I said, hearing the wardrobe start to crack and splinter.

Connie glanced back towards the sound of breaking wood and threw another vial at the wall. Green liquid splashed onto the brick and ate through, melting it like butter. The room on the other side was dark.

I pulled the bathroom door closed and we ran. Connie tripped on something and swore, scrambling to her feet.

"Careful, I smashed another bottle," she said. "The floor's covered in ice."

"It'll make us harder to follow," I said.

Getting over sheet ice in the dark isn't the easiest thing I've ever done. I slipped and fell twice, crawling on all fours until I found something to pull myself to my feet. Then I ran some more, slipped, and decided to crawl the rest of the way, my hands burning from the ice.

Hargreaves voice came from the other room.

"Search the bedchambers," he said. "They must be here."

One of the other voices sounded like they were disagreeing.

"Search them, damn you," Hargreaves snapped. "If they've vanished, so be it, but it won't be for lack of searching."

"Esteban," Connie hissed. "This way."

I dug my fingernails into the ice and propelled myself towards her voice. A shaft of light burst into the room. Hargreaves stood behind us, framed in the hole melted by Connie's alchemy.

"There, take them!" he shouted, stepping onto the ice...

...and standing firm. He paused, slid, and got his bearings, a smile spreading over his features as he bounded across the room towards me.

"Hostia!" I groaned, and let Connie pull me through the door.

She slammed it and toppled a pile of boxes in front of it. They were mostly empty, but they'd take a moment to climb.

Hargreaves hit the door like a rhino. Modern doors aren't made of wood, not all the way. This one looked like it was mostly cardboard internally. Hargreaves smashed it into two pieces, hurtling through and into the boxes.

"Argh, dammit!" he yelled, tripping and falling over the boxes.

He was sure footed. He tripped, caught himself, and hopped, overbalanced but not falling.

The room was another storeroom, lit by skylights. It looked like it was going to be a tanning salon one day – upright tanning booths stood amongst the other brick-a-brac – I ran backwards through the room, Connie guiding me by the collar, throwing anything she could see into his path.

Hargreaves chased at full speed, leaping like a

championship hurdler.

"Esteban, this way," Connie shouted, and let go of my collar.

I turned and ran. I'm squat and heavy with short legs. I'd done more exercise in the last day than I'd done in the last six months, but even then, I was pleased to say that Connie wasn't too far ahead of me.

Alright... it's true she was keeping down with me, but let me have this moment.

There was another part-painted corridor beyond the tanning room, with open doors on either side. The air here was heavy with the smell of wet paint and there were still cloths on the floor, tangling my feet as I ran.

"Here," Connie said.

She dashed through another door and stood, holding it open.

All the while, I could feel the weight of Hargreaves' bounding footsteps chasing behind me. He was breathing hard, but he had longer legs. I put everything I had into a last burst of speed. My head went down as I threw myself towards the door–

And nearly choked as Hargreaves' rough hand grabbed my collar. He must have just planted his feet and used his weight to stop my momentum. I snapped back, the neck of my t-shirt breaking as Hargreaves pulled on it with all his strength.

My feet flew out and the world tilted. I crashed back onto the floor hard enough to knock the breath out of me and I lay there stunned.

Hargreaves gave me a savage kick in the shoulder. I

was lucky he didn't manage to get my head.

"Got you, you little–" he started to say.

A glass tube shattered against his shoulder. He screamed and melted into black goo, bursting into a shower of magical sparks as he vanished.

"Hostia..." I said, lying there, gasping.

Connie helped me. I was glad I hadn't eaten anything. If I had all this running would have made me sick.

"Can we just say I'm fit now...?" I said, managing to smile.

The house was silent. If any of the bailiffs had followed Hargreaves, they hadn't made it much further than the storeroom where Connie had covered the floor in ice.

I stood still for a while with my heart pounding so hard it sounded like it was going to burst out of my chest.

Connie beckoned me through the door and pushed it so it was almost closed. The room was dark, with the windows hidden behind big, empty wardrobes that looked like they either been taken out of, or were waiting to be put into, the guest rooms.

"That's it, I haven't got anything else," Connie said.

"Can you make more?" I asked.

"Yes," Connie said, and I think I could see her white hair move as she nodded in the half light. "But we should get out of here."

"We must be on the far side of the farm. We're close to the road," I whispered.

I could see Connie nodding from the way her bright white hair bobbed in the semi-darkness. A car whooshed past just outside the window.

A smile crept across my face. We just needed to get out of the window and onto the main road and we'd be reunited with Aunt Vanessa.

"My grandmother can deal with this," I whispered. "I don't care how busy Aunt Vanessa thinks she is, this is out of my league."

Connie gave me a hurt look. I'd never realised before, but she was so pale that she glowed in the darkness.

"It's not that bad," she said.

"Alright, you do it," I said. "Between you and Danny you've done everything so far. I'm just the transport. I'm not an Archmage. Time Magic is useless for this sort of thing."

Connie looked back at me. Her shades made it look like the dark was eating her face.

"What?" Connie whispered. "Stopping another Chronomancer?"

"She's a revenant," I said, raising my voice more than I should have. "Skill doesn't count against brute force."

Connie took the sort of in-breath that suggested she was going speak. Then something truly horrible happened.

Most people can't tell when they've been chopped and messed around with in time. If normal people, even sorcerers, have their time frozen they just can't tell.

Someone appears where they weren't a second ago. The furniture moves. At most, they'll be sensitive enough to get a bit of a headache.

For a Chronomancer it feels like being buried in a block of rubber.

Time stopped around us. I could feel the wrongness of Jennet's magic. I tried moving back and forward to get myself out of her reach, but she was too strong. She kept time clamped around me in a death grip.

She walked in and sauntered around the dark room, picking a suitable spot. She looked around, smiling at me, and conjured six bailiffs out of the shadows. Finally, she brought Hargreaves back, dragging him out of the past.

"Where are they?" Hargreaves asked, looking.

"Wait," the little girl said. "I need to–"

"Show them to me now," Hargreaves said, tersely. "They have to be arrested and brought to justice."

"Not yet," Jennet said.

"Show them to me," Hargreaves demanded. "You know what happens."

"I brought you here," the little said.

The bailiffs shifted threateningly.

She restarted time.

"Connie!" I said.

I grabbed her arm and tried to pull her away. One of the bailiffs hit me in the stomach with a cudgel. It was the second time I was glad I hadn't eaten. I doubled over with spots in front of my eyes.

"Stop," Connie said, putting a hand on my shoulder.

"It's alright."

"You are under arrest in the name of the King," Hargreaves said. "To be examined on suspicion of witchcraft."

I tried to shift time again. The little girl held me tight.

"Esteban," Connie said, squeezing my shoulder. "It's alright. They won't hurt us...yet."

Chapter Nine

I was numb with fear as the bailiffs took us out of the house. I remember them being freaked out by all the strange gadgets and potions they passed in the rooms and bathrooms, making dark remarks about witches' laboratories. It was funny when one of them identified Aunt Vanessa's face cream as 'ointment from the flesh of unborn babes'.

"Where will we be brought to trial?" Connie asked.

The little girl led the way, with Hargreaves holding her hand.

"First you'll be up in front of Roger Nowell," Hargreaves said. "And then you'll go to the Assizes at Lancaster castle."

He turned, grinning.

"And from there, ye'll be hanged."

I bit back a sarcastic comment. There was a chance the little girl would run out of power before then. Even I knew that Assize courts only happened two or three times a year back in the time of these trials.

"Do you mind if I ask what year it is? My friend and I have lost track."

"Not at all," Hargreaves said. "You have found yourselves in Lancashire, in the year of Our Lord 1612."

"That makes sense," I said, looking over to Connie, he pushed her shades tighter onto her face.

The bailiffs kept us surrounded, not that it mattered. I was overmatched and Connie was out of supplies.

It was only when they led us into the yard that I saw the first glimmer of light: five more bailiffs waiting for us – but no sign of Aunt Vanessa or Danny.

"No sign of the others?" Hargreaves asked.

The bailiffs shook their heads.

"We gave chase, sir, but they vanished," one said.

I tried not to show the ideas firing in my head. I couldn't help wondering about the range of the little girl's powers.

I tried to think of a landmark on the road.

"Alack," I said, trying to imitate their speech. "They led you not to our home in the blasted oak?"

The bailiff shook his head.

"Nay," he said. "They disappeared from us before they got to the second gate."

I tried to work out how far that was from the farmhouse. It was good – the little girl did have limitations. Her time spell had a range. Unfortunately, it was a range of about a two minute run.

"Maybe out on open ground..." I muttered.

"What?" asked the bailiff.

"Nothing," I said. "I'm sorry."

The bailiff gave me a suspicious look.

"Ye will be," he said.

"Where will you take us now?" I asked.

Hargreaves looked back at us.

"We'll walk you into the village and you'll be held at the gaol until the next delivery," Hargreaves said.

"Then you'll be on the wagon to Lancaster castle."

Connie frowned.

"How far is that?" she asked. "Please, my feet are sore from running."

"I'm sorry for it," Hargreaves said. "They must have soft grass in hell. You'll walk another hour or two into the village and thence you can rest until the Assizes."

Connie's phone vibrated in my pocket. At some point, it had been shoved into my jacket, coming to life as somebody texted it. Once I was sure they were all looking at Connie, I sneaked a look at the screen, hoping it wouldn't just be an advert for pizza.

It was a text from Danny. It read, 'WE R COMING, HOLD US IN TIME.'

I felt something heavy hurtling down the hill. Unopposed, the little girl would have avoided it; she would just have folded time around us so that it stayed in the present and we didn't. I clung onto her. I couldn't move her, but I could stop her moving.

Aunt Vanessa's Land rover exploded through the hedge, wallowing in the air before landing with a crash in the middle of the group of bailiffs. Headlights and floodlights flared into life, blinding them.

The little girl tried to fold time around us, locking us in a bubble of 1612. I leapt on her spell with all my strength and tried to paralyse it. We struggled, and silver needles of spiritual pain stabbed through my fingers.

She was stronger than me in every way. But you don't always need to be stronger; sometimes you just need to be strong enough.

Danny rammed one of the 4x4's side doors into a bailiff's face, causing him to burst and vanish into the past.

Aunt Vanessa grabbed me by the shoulders and dragged me away.

"This way," she said, towing me by the hand. "Run."

The bailiffs threw themselves into chasing us. Connie screamed – more an angry scream than a frightened scream – as one of them grabbed her by the hair. Then she twisted around to punch him hard in the face. Surprisingly, that wasn't enough to make him vanish.

Looking back, Connie was surrounded by five of the six bailiffs and standing right next Jennet. I squirmed out of Aunt Vanessa's grip and made a run back through them.

It's hard to stop time for long. Even when no one is trying to fight me, it wants to move, and eventually it just starts to slip through your fingers. Even someone as powerful as Jennet couldn't stop time leaking out and doing its own thing.

But that's the difference between power and training: you don't have to completely stop time. You can slow it down so much that it might as well have stopped, which is much, much easier.

I stretched time out as far as I could, turning one second into about half a minute, and ran between the bailiffs. I looked like a streak of movement to them, which wasn't going to do much good for my reputation as a witch and creature of Satan.

The two in front moved quick enough to start turning their heads towards me as I hurried past, praying I could get to a point where this trip wouldn't include any more running. The middle two darted into my path. They were fast enough that I could see they were moving, but not fast enough to stop me.

The last two had stepped right in front of Connie the minute the rescue had started. I took a wide path around them, sauntering around the back, where Connie had started to throw herself backwards, moving like glacier.

The little girl and Hargreaves stared at me. She was too strong for me to just loop Connie into the spell. I reached out to grab Connie's sleeve so that I could physically drag her into my magic—

And I missed. The world flickered: I'd gone straight past, with Connie behind me.

I turned around and reached out for her again. The bailiffs had moved in a single jump, almost surrounding us now. I moved as fast as I could, putting everything into my spe—

The world flickered again. The bailiffs weren't running towards us, they were swarming over Connie, four of them had grabbed a limb each, with another standing between Connie and me. They were still moving in super slow motion, so slowly that they barely seemed to be moving unless you knew. I was being cut out of time.

I felt a cold wash of panic in my stomach. The little girl was moving at the same slow speed as the bailiffs but she was looking straight at me. She was throwing me around in time. I don't think even my grandmother could do that, and she's probably the best Chronomancer alive.

Then again, the little girl wasn't alive. She was a revenant. And she had brute strength.

She must have seen the look on my face as I was thinking. I felt her lash out with magic. It was savage and sharp. She severed straight through my spell, sending me sprawling on the ground as time snapped back to normal.

Connie screamed and bit as they dragged her back. It wasn't frightened screaming. It was anger.

Unfortunately, anger doesn't matter if you're fighting four people, not if they're all bigger than you are.

Then again, I had my own problems.

The man standing in front of Connie leapt on me as I fell. He had his arms wrapped around me before my head had stopped spinning and started lifting me off the ground. The little girl was still holding time, and I could feel her ready to spring if I tried to use magic again.

I reached out as far as I could and found a car that was driving too fast. I dragged it through time and threw it into the little girl's bubble of the 17th century.

The car screamed around the bend with a roar of engines. Music thumped through its stereo. Headlights filled the road. The bailiff holding me screamed and let go, covering his eyes.

I rolled away and got to my feet, letting go of the

car. The little girl held it where it was.

All this happened in a split second. She cut me down when I instinctively tried to stretch time.

It was the force of the backlash that saved my life. The car hit the bailiff at a mad speed, sending him back where he'd come from in a shower of magical energy. It would have hit me. The rebound from the little girl cancelling my spell saved me.

The backlash knocked me away. The car hit me on the thigh, spinning me around and hurling me into the embankment. I managed to get an arm up to protect my head. A rock smashed my elbow instead of my skull.

The car sped past and vanished.

I screamed for Danny. Jennet looked at me, smiled, and laughed a disgustingly cute little girl laugh. I wondered how long it would be before the four bailiffs decided they only needed three to hang onto Connie and one of them came after me.

Hargreaves was older, but even he could take me down, being honest.

On the other hand, Hargreaves was more interested in Connie than in me. She was biting down hard, and kicking like a mule. Her shades had slipped enough to show the strange light behind them and Hargreaves was shouting at his men to cover her eyes.

It would have been the perfect chance for me to try to rescue her again… but I had nothing. I clambered off the embankment and stood there, too scared to call out to her, but too ashamed to run away. The little girl watched me. She didn't even look evil now. She smiled and giggled at me as Connie thrashed.

Danny and Aunt Vanessa stood where they'd got out of the Land Rover, looking as helpless and uncertain as I did. I could see the numbers flashing behind Danny's eyes as his mind went through everything he could do and came up with nothing repeatedly.

I don't know why I even looked at Aunt Vanessa. Aunt Vanessa just seemed so... nice... that I didn't think she'd have the nerve to do anything.

My Aunt's eyes flashed with dangerous, cold fire. It sounds like an exaggeration, but I've seen my grandmother do some frightening things with expression.

Aunt Vanessa slammed the car door and stalked towards the little girl.

"You," Aunt Vanessa said, jabbing a finger in the air towards the girl. "Stop this."

The little girl turned to look at her, obvious surprise on her face.

"Jennet Device," Aunt Vanessa said. "I know your name. Look, I'm sorry we gave the answer we gave, I truly am, but that's no reason to do this."

Jennet looked between us. She was unreadable.

"Look," Aunt Vanessa squatted down so she was on the little girl's level. "I'm honestly sorry that Esteban said something so stupid. Esteban and me, our family's a bit... different. Our family isn't even the way yours is. We'd never betray my mother because I can't imagine anyone I fear more."

"Oi, that's not fair," I said.

Aunt Vanessa gave me a savage look and shook her head.

"Please," she turned back to the little girl. "Let our friend go. Take me if you want to, but please, our friend hasn't done anything to you."

Jennet frowned, lost in thought.

"Mister Hargreaves?" she asked.

"Aye?" he asked, looking distracted.

The little girl held his hand so tightly that his flesh was white.

"Have you got those other bailiffs? The men from the village?" she asked.

Hargreaves looked at her and shook his head as if he was trying to clear it.

"Aye," he said. "They should have come across the field by now, God knows where they are."

I felt the little girl reach out through time. For the first time, I felt her power waiver, but she was strong and I was tired. She reached into the 17th century, and dragged people into the present.

Shouting voices rang out in the dark behind the house.

"They're here," Hargreaves shouted. "Come around the house and give a hand."

Connie thrashed desperately, but they were too strong for her. Panic and fear made me feel like I was being dunked in ice water.

People were running in the dark, and getting closer.

"Connie…" I said, staring at her. "Connie… I'm sorry."

Connie stopped struggling and looked straight at me. She jerked her head around and managed to get her mouth free. My stomach turned as she spoke.

"Fawkes," she said. "Go!"

So I ran. I ran past Danny and Aunt Vanessa and scrambled over the gate into the field on the other side.

Behind me, footsteps thundered through the night.

I heard the little girl's voice. She wasn't shouting, but it still seemed impossibly loud.

"They're heading towards the water," she said. "Swim the witches!"

Chapter Ten

I could hear that Danny and Aunt Vanessa were running with me, which made me hate myself less for leaving Connie. In the distance, I could hear sounds of yelling and smashing that meant bailiffs from the 17th century were destroying Aunt V's Land Rover.

I barely felt the run up to the top of the hill. Fear and adrenaline carried me straight up to the top as Danny streaked past me. Aunt Vanessa was last, trailing at the back, too close to the bailiffs for comfort.

I could hear the bailiffs spread out in the field – they'd vaulted the gate and now they were catching up with us. Danny was ahead but he kept on looking back, slowing down to wait for us.

"Danny, go," I shouted.

"We're not leaving anyone else," he shouted back. "Come one."

We could hear them on the left and right. We crested the hill and started on the downward slope.

The moonlight reflected on a fast moving river. It caught the surface, highlighting the black water with silver. It was just about narrow enough that I might be able to jump it, so long as I could grab something on the other bank and drag myself out of the water.

The bailiffs behind me were still further away than the ones on the right and left. I put my head down and powered towards the water's edge.

I was almost there when I realized they'd tricked us. They'd curved around the base of the hill and got in front of us. The others had just been herding us towards a trap.

"Danny, if you've got a new friend, this is the time," I said.

Aunt Vanessa gave a muffled scream as one of them quietly ran up behind her and tackled her to the ground. I had just enough time to yelp and jump to the left as another tried to dive-tackle me. I heard a shout and a splash that told me Danny had managed to dump one of his into the river.

Two of them leapt on Aunt Vanessa. They were all around us, the only difference had been that the ones on the right and left had been shouting, while the ones behind us ran as quickly and quietly as they could.

Desperation gave me strength. For the first time, I broke the spell on the two holding Aunt Vanessa. They faded back into their own time and vanished. We were far away here, and Jennet was weaker, but it still felt as if the bailiffs were everywhere.

Two more bailiffs came running for Aunt Vanessa, who scrambled to her feet and dragged me towards the river. One of them made a leap for her and she punched him squarely in the face, sending him staggering backwards.

Danny leapt the river, landing a few feet short of the other bank. The water grabbed him and he shot down stream, moving with the flow until he could drag himself out onto dry land.

Aunt Vanessa jumped after him, vanishing into the water with a splash. I was suddenly really, glad that I could swim.

For about a second.

I was taking my run up to jump when they caught me. They didn't mess around: four people leapt on me and pinned me to the ground. I struggled uselessly, but they were four full-grown men who worked on the land, there was no chance I was getting free.

"Your friends have abandoned you," said one of the bailiffs.

After a second, I realized it was one of the men from Malkin Tower, the Device Family Cottage.

I could just about see Aunt Vanessa and Danny on the other side of the river, looking worried.

The bailiffs didn't know they existed. We must have reached the edge of Jennet Device's power range. She couldn't stretch her magic far enough to reach the far bank of the river. I closed my eyes and hoped.

"Please, sir," I said. "They were destroyed by the water."

"Bah," said the bailiff. "Rubbish, everyone knows a witch floats."

"Swim the witch!" shouted another.

"We haven't got a rope," said the bailiff.

Aunt Vanessa and Danny were less than ten feet away. I let myself be dragged to my feet. There weren't as many bailiffs as I'd thought – maybe ten at most – but they were still twice my size and brawny.

"We can use a stick," said another bailiff.

"I don't see why we have to swim them anyway," my bailiff said. "We don't swim witches in these parts, we scratch them."

"Hargreaves wanted 'em swum," said the other bailiff. "So swum they'll be."

My bailiff kept a firm hold on my collar and glowered resentfully.

"Aye, alright then," he said. "Fetch a stick."

The moors are sparse, but they aren't a desert. I tried not to look too directly at where Danny and Aunt Vanessa were standing, hoping Jennet wouldn't come any closer, or think of a way to extend her power.

With any luck, they were having enough problems with Connie.

I looked at my feet and tried to look hopeless. It didn't take much acting.

I heard a woody snap in the darkness. Two of the bailiffs came back laughing with a tree branch.

"Here we are," one said. "This'll do. It's got a fork at the end and nothing to hold on to."

He offered a ten-foot sapling, snapped off at the base. They'd torn the shoots off the side to leave just a fork in the top. Despite my misery and fear, it was a shame they'd killed a tree so they could drown me.

My bailiff watched them, holding my collar tightly. His face was cold and serious, locked into an angry frown. He stood slightly in front of me as they came closer.

"He's to be taken for trial," my bailiff said.

"Aye," said another. "And so he will be. Once we know he's a witch."

They reached around my bailiff and dragged me to

the water's edge. One of them took my jacket off and threw it onto the ground, shoving me ankle deep into the water. It was ice cold, despite the warm weather.

"Alright, boy," a bailiff said, putting a hand on my back. "If you sink, then you were innocent and God have mercy on your soul. If the water rejects you, you're a witch, and we take you for trial. Understand?"

I looked up at him. He had dark hair and blue eyes. If he'd been slightly cleaner, and not trying to kill me, he would have been quite handsome.

"What's your name?" I asked.

"Pah!" he said. "I'll not give you power over me."

Then he shoved me into the water as hard as he could.

I managed a deep breath as the water took me. The river was quite narrow, more of a stream really, but it was fast, and rocky. My instinct was to panic and claw at the water in front of me. I wanted more than anything to take another breath, but I held it and forced myself to try to swim properly.

The forked stick hit me in the middle of my back and pushed me deeper into the water. I managed not to lose any air by crying out in surprise. I bobbed back up and they pushed me down again. The water was carrying me fast. A rock hit me in the side, the same place I was clipped by the car. The pain made colors flash in front of my eyes.

I managed to fight my way to the surface long enough to get half a breath before they shoved me down again. Stones hit me and scraped along as I bounced down the river. I flailed my arms and forced myself to try to swim again, my mind screaming in panic.

"This is why we need a bloody rope!" my bailiff shouted.

I could hear they were running to keep up with me, and so were Danny and Aunt Vanessa on the other side. I heard Aunt Vanessa shout my name but for some reason I couldn't talk.

They hit me with the stick again. I think they were trying to hook it around my neck and drag me out of the water. They managed to get me around the shoulders, but the stick wasn't as strong as they'd thought it was and one of the forks snapped, sending me under again.

I breathed out this time. I couldn't stop myself. I took in a lungful of water and coughed it back out again, my lungs burning, but then I heaved in another great lungful of cold river water. I choked and lost control of my arms and legs, flailing around under the water, sinking as I was carried along with the tide.

More rocks hit me, but I could barely feel them or anything else by now. I couldn't hear the sounds of the bailiffs or my friends. The pain of the cold water hitting my throat and lungs faded into a distant dullness.

I was literally about to drown.

Then things changed.

The river picked me up and threw me hard against the far bank. One minute the water was crushing me. Then it was like a living thing, lifting me high above the bailiffs and slamming me hard against the dry land.

I landed on the opposite side of the river from the bailiffs. I couldn't move and coughing the water up was worse than swallowing it in the first place.

My first breath was like pouring lemon juice onto a cut. My throat was tight and I still couldn't make a sound. The only thing I could really think about was the moon. It was huge. It filled the sky, so close I could make out craters and furrows on the surface. If the moon ever really got that close there would probably have been floods and disasters... then again, the water had just picked me up and thrown me onto dry land, so things weren't normal.

Aunt Vanessa shouted something and Jennet Device shouted something back. Danny's voice cut through everything.

It wasn't a normal voice. It wasn't loud, but I could have heard it if I'd still have been on the riverbed. My head was still a fog of pain and oxygen starvation, but his words cut through everything.

"Lunariel, Angel of the Moon, Left Eye of the Wedjt, Lord of Time, Scribe of the Gods. By My Lord, Patron, and all the Choirs of Angels, hear me. Lunariel, gate of Dreams and Gate of Ivory, I call to you. Lunariel: This. Should. Not. Be. Here."

Then, suddenly, the moonlight burned. Not like fire, more like getting something on your skin that gives you a rash. It wasn't great, but at least I was too tired to scratch.

For Jennet and the bailiffs, it was different. The moonlight lit them up with a white flame. They lost their human appearance immediately, turning into pale shapes with no eyes, ears or mouth. They burned with a white hot fire, vanishing into nothingness.

I think that was the bit where I passed out for a while.

Chapter Eleven

When I came to, someone had propped me up against a wall. The moon was back to its normal size. Everything hurt.

"I'm alive, aren't I?"

Danny laughed, but without any real feeling. Aunt Vanessa looked worried. Over her shoulder, I could see that the bailiffs had wrecked the house, although some of that might have been Connie and me. Most of the front windows were smashed, and the Land rover was just scrap. Sadly, they hadn't touched the bikes.

"What was that?" I asked, and climbed to my feet.

Danny looked serious.

"My new friend, Lunariel, Angel of the Moon. Good for controlling water and cancelling wicked magic," he said. "I think I owe him now."

I nodded.

"Did you see what happened to Connie?" I asked.

Danny shook his head.

"We don't know," he said. "We looked everywhere, but there's no sign."

"I don't understand it," Aunt Vanessa said. "Why would she have disappeared at the same time as the others?"

I glanced at Danny. We exchanged a look of mutual dread.

"Connie made a deal with a spirit," Danny said,

looking at Aunt Vanessa. "A long time ago… it's possibly why she isn't here."

"Oh. You mean they're the same?" Aunt Vanessa asked.

Danny gave her a look of irritation.

"What's that supposed to mean?" he asked. "Anyway, she's not exactly the same. I might have sent them back to the same place, though."

"First things first, we need to find out where that would be," I said. "And that means talking to someone who knows what happened next."

Danny nodded unwillingly, looking around in the darkness. Aunt Vanessa watched him, looking equally unhappy.

She took out an energy bar and started nibbling on it.

"Look, I've got to ask. That huge moon spirit—" she asked.

"Don't," Danny said. "Every spirit wants something different. My main one, Medimiel, wants me to read books. Sometimes I have to buy one and sacrifice it to him. Lunariel... it's more physical."

Aunt Vanessa frowned. It made me angry with my grandmother: she obviously hadn't bothered teaching Auntie Vee the basics of the magical world.

"It probably wants either flesh or blood," I said. "Even the planetary Angels can get a bit funny sometimes."

Danny shook his head.

"He wants one thing, mate," Danny said. "Everything he does for me costs one night under the moon."

"What?" I asked. "That doesn't sound so bad."

Danny gave me a disappointed look.

"Think about it, mate: he appears as a huge full moon, and wants me to spend a night running under the moon. Do you think he's just worried about my fitness?" Danny asked.

The penny dropped.

"Hostia…" I said.

Aunt Vanessa looked between us.

"What?" She asked, frowning.

I glanced at Danny.

"It wants him to run under the moon," I said. "But not as a human… I think it wants to turn him into a werewolf."

Danny shrugged. The night air was starting to go straight through my soaking wet clothes. Aunt Vanessa was visibly shivering. So was I.

"The house doesn't look good, does it?" I asked.

"Our stuff wouldn't have been there if it was," Danny said, then saw the look on my face. "What?"

"…you weren't there," I said. "In fact, it didn't like the sound of you."

Danny and Aunt Vanessa both turned to look at me. Danny raised an eyebrow.

"What wasn't?" he asked.

"I thought it was your new friend, or a projection from Jennet," I said. "Some kind of dog-thing came and gave our luggage back."

Chapter Twelve

We were back in the kitchen. The lights were still working. One of the windows was broken after the fight with the Bailiffs, but we'd managed to get the furniture back where it should have been.

"Demons are old," Danny said. "They move through time and they change as they get older. It's not a demon."

I sat in my dry, warm clothes feeling vaguely guilty. But we didn't have a plan and running around getting pneumonia wasn't going to do Connie any good. Danny and Aunt Vanessa sat behind steaming mugs of coffee.

"What about the spirit?" Danny asked.

"I don't know," I said. "It was bigger and nastier than me; it felt like Jennet, but not quite. It wasn't even travelling through time. Everywhere I was, it was there too."

Danny watched me. In films, they try to show the minds of bright people working. When Danny is thinking it's like watching someone spearfishing: not moving, sitting patiently over a fast-flowing river… then BAM - it's done.

"Did you get rid of it?" he asked.

"Yeah," I said, shifting in my seat. "I couldn't do anything. I couldn't even move… then Connie did something with salt."

Danny smiled.

"Just salt? Did she do an invocation?" Danny asked, leaning closer.

"She said something in Enochian, but I didn't understand it," I said.

"The spirit didn't like that?" Danny asked. "Did Connie draw any special shapes around him, or was it just a triangle?"

I must have given him a blank look, because he switched into explain-it-to-the-moron-mode.

"Think about it," Danny said, turning to Aunt Vanessa. "Because suddenly what you were saying makes sense."

Aunt Vanessa looked confused.

"What do you mean, 'what I was saying'?" she asked.

"Esteban, do you get it?" Danny asked.

"Oh..." I said.

Danny smiled. He cupped his hands around his coffee and tilted his chair back when he saw the look of recognition on my face. I couldn't help smiling with him. Aunt Vanessa looked between us, tired and irritated.

"Look, just tell me," she snapped. "I've had enough of this. Sorcerers aren't better than anyone else."

"Alright," Danny said, putting his hands out calmingly. "What Connie did doesn't do anything to get rid of demons. I'm a full time conjurer and I couldn't get rid of one without a tonne of prep. I might be wrong... but I think what Connie did was a spell to get rid of the dead."

Aunt Vanessa looked confused again.

"Another revenant?" she asked.

Danny nodded.

"Yeah," he said. "And now the fairy ring makes sense. There was more than one person doing magic. That's a lot of power."

Danny smiled again, and gulped at his coffee.

"You see," he said. "Just like that, your day picks up."

Aunt Vanessa looked annoyed again.

"Look, are you going to tell me what's going on?" she asked.

Danny rolled his eyes.

"More than one of the Device family was doing magic," he said. "And he might have become a revenant like Jennet."

I nodded. Things were starting to make sense.

"You think that dog was James Device? He seemed a bit thick…" I said.

Danny gulped the last of his coffee down and went for the door. Opening it let in the chilly night air. Even now, I was dry and wearing warm clothes, the fingers of cold got under my skin. Aunt Vanessa scowled and got up to follow him. Danny looked back at me.

"Being undead sorts out a lot of problems, mate," Danny said. "And all it takes to be a revenant is emotion and magic. If he wants to talk to you, we might be able to ask him what Jennet wants, but first we need to be sure."

Ideas were fizzing through my head. I nodded slowly.

"And by 'sure', you mean ask someone who's been dead for nearly four hundred years?" I asked.

Danny nodded. Aunt Vanessa put up a hand.

"If we now think salt works against revenants, is there anything else?" she asked.

I looked at Danny. He narrowed his eyes thoughtfully.

"Iron might, but it would have to be cold forged," he said.

Aunt Vanessa rolled her eyes.

"Oh that's just rubbish," she said. "Cold Iron just means 'iron'. Any iron that hasn't been turned into steel."

I wondered if she was right. It was more hope than I'd had in a while.

"Tell you what," he said. "Get that horseshoe from above the door. We're going to speak to Jennet Device before she died."

Chapter Thirteen

We cycled through the night, mostly over fields on the way to the farmhouse. It felt like the whole ride was uphill. Logically, that meant the way back should have been downhill. It wasn't. Thankfully, my bike turned out to have witchcraft and devilry: Danny taught me that mountain bikes have gears and how to shift. I could suddenly ride my bike up hills with it only *nearly* killing me.

The moon was still huge in the sky. That was good: the fields we were riding through were hilly and some were crossed by crumbling stone walls.

The moonlight didn't make the cottage look sinister, it looked magical. The fields were full of night-scented plants that attracted moths. Despite the only light being pale moonlight the cool air was still full of insects like a summer's day. It might have been because it was dark, but the air was full of the sickly sweet smell of flowers.

Danny got off his bike gracefully. Aunt Vanessa has been riding for most of her life. I was pleased with myself for managing to actually get off it instead of just pulling the brakes, panicking and falling onto the grass.

Danny got a paper bag out of his pocket.

"Wear these, but be careful, because they may not work," Danny said.

I couldn't see what he gave me, but it felt like a ring.

I slipped it on my finger and motioned for Aunt Vanessa to do the same.

"Rings?" Aunt Vanessa asked, squinting in the moonlight.

I tried to look knowing, slightly relieved that she'd asked the question so I didn't have to.

"Iron rings," Danny said. "They should protect you a bit from revenant magic… but I don't know how much. If at all. I didn't think they'd do anything."

"That's comforting," Aunt Vanessa said.

He led us back to the cottage, gesturing for us to follow him inside. I could still feel the echo of what had happened when we'd first met Jennet. What was left didn't do much to shield us from the cold wind, but the air definitely felt different in there. I'm usually really sensitive to magic, but it was hard to get a feeling for it here. I looked at Danny and Aunt Vanessa, wondering if they could even feel it at all.

"Alright… Vanessa? Could you tell Esteban what you know about Jennet Device?" Danny asked. "Even if we can't find out where James is and have a chat with him, we can talk to her."

Aunt Vanessa's lip quivered. She looked tired and like she was going to burst into tears at any moment.

"She didn't die as a little girl," Aunt Vanessa said. "She gave up the rest of the family in court. Then she lived until she was nearly thirty. She died in prison, after someone accused her of being a witch."

"That's irony," Danny said. "Full on irony."

I frowned.

"This is starting to feel like a bad idea. Doing time magic hasn't gone well for us lately," I said.

"You can't learn without failing," he replied.

"…is this going to get Connie back?" I asked.

Danny's smile faltered.

"I don't know mate. We don't even know where she is. As far as ideas go, this is it. Besides, we can't have a revenant chasing us for the rest of our lives."

He was right. There was no point running around shouting about it, we needed information.

In fact, there was a chance Lunariel's power might just have blasted Connie out of existence.

I nodded. Aunt Vanessa had walked away and was watching us worriedly, chewing her knuckle.

"Are you alright, Auntie Vee?" I asked.

She shook her head.

"No," she said. "There should be something I can do."

I tried to smile.

"I'm not sure there's anything any of us can do," I said.

She looked up at me.

"Yes, but you're kids. I'm thirty-seven years old. I run an archaeology unit, and I'm the only reason you're here…," she said, her voice breaking as she spoke. "And now you're trying to sort it out and I'm just watching…"

She put her face in her hands and started sobbing.

Danny looked like he was going to go over to her. I shook my head.

"No time," I said, quietly. "Let's just do the work."

Danny looked between Aunt Vanessa and me. He gave me a look I've never seen before.

"What?" I asked.

"Nah," he said, shaking himself. "It's only natural."

"What do you mean?"

"You and your grandmother," Danny said. "I always thought you were really different."

I looked at Aunt Vanessa, crying quietly. Her whole body was shaking from the force of it.

"I don't see what else we can do," I said. "Even this might blow up in our faces, and we don't know what's happening to Connie. Look, give Auntie V a cuddle or something if you want, but be ready in case something tries to drag us off as witches."

Danny went over to Aunt Vanessa, looking at me as if I was a stranger.

I took a breath and pushed back into the past. There's nothing worse than when time is soft and easily stirred up. It's like the muddy silt on the bottom of a river: even if you only move a little bit, the water goes cloudy and you can't see anything. That's what time is like all over Pendle Hill. I looked back carefully, pushing through a year at a time and waiting for the chaos to settle: I went back to last year, and a huge rack of lights appeared, with ghostly people digging in the cottage; another three or four and some people were sitting in the overgrown shell of the house, listening to music.

Further back and I saw a tramp appear in the corner

of the room. The walls had been higher then, and he'd been sheltering from the wind. Danny looked at him, then at me, as he appeared in the present.

I'll bet people saw many ghosts around Pendle.

I didn't look back any further for a couple of minutes, until the tramp had disappeared, and then pressed on, looking back through time year by year.

I saw Jennet as a revenant. My heart skipped a beat. She looked at where I was, like the men in Hobb's Field. I didn't dare breath. She frowned and looked past me. The men had thrown a rock. She could do much worse.

I could just stop looking, but I'd have to look again, and that would be a mistake. It's the sort of thing that happens in ghost stories: imagine you get a feeling that someone's watching you and someone knocks on the door. It might just be wind, but what if someone knocks on the window as well?

That's what it's like being a Chronomancer where someone is looking back through time. A weird feeling in one corner might be imagination, but two would be suspicious. Jennet watched me for a minute. Then she walked away.

I looked further, even more carefully. I reached the 17th century: 1699, 1670, 1643, 1636… and I suddenly couldn't even remember what period I was looking for.

This was going to be the hard part: speaking to someone in the present while looking back into the past and not losing sight of what I was looking at. Looking back is easier than full time travel, but I'd still have to disrupt time and hope that the little girl didn't notice me... again.

"Guys... when did you say Jennet Device really died?" I asked.

Maybe I just tuned out for a moment, but it seemed like instantly, Aunt Vanessa was in the middle of explaining something.

"...then records show that she was still in the castle after the trial date," Aunt Vanessa was saying.

"What date?" I asked. "Give me a last time period I should be looking for."

Aunt Vanessa thought for a moment. I tried not to lose my vision of the past.

"1632," Aunt Vanessa said. "She probably won't be around much after then. If you can tell what date it is."

I realised, with surprise, that I could. The little girl was in and out of the house a lot between 1635 and 1632. I didn't see any humans, but then she'd just walk in, look around, and then disappear. It took me a while to realise she was probably looking through time too.

I'd never seen another Chronomancer doing magic. Even my grandmother never really let me see her working unless it was an exercise for my apprenticeship.

The Device house came to life. A fire lit the hearth and all the shelves were full of pots again. There were crumbs of cheese on the table and there was bread in a ceramic tub kept next to the fireplace. It wasn't rich, but it wasn't as poor as the Device family had been when we'd last seen the place.

There was a woman wearing a brown dress with an orange-red skirt. She was about twenty years older than I'd ever seen her, but there was no mistaking her face: she was Jennet Device as an adult.

"I've got her," I said. "What shall we do?"

"Can you show her to me?" Danny asked.

I was about to try when Jennet Device looked straight at me. It wasn't even the sort of look you'd give a strange person in strange clothes who had just appeared in your house: it was a straight out look of recognition. I felt time warp slightly around her.

"Hello…" she said, picking up a knife. "When do you come from?"

"Danny mate?" I asked. "I think we might have a problem."

Danny raised an eyebrow. In the past, Jennet Device marched across the room, a blunt, but still dangerous, knife in her hand.

"Are you another bloody traveller? Come to gawp at the witch?" she snapped. "How would you like it? Everyone whispering. Maybe I should follow you home so that all your posh friends know what you do."

I closed my time sight with a wave of feedback. The fabric of time broke and whirled. Rogue time hit Danny and Aunt Vanessa: streaks of white shot through Danny's dreads; the edges of Aunt Vanessa's coat tattered and flaked.

"Mate?" Danny asked. "What's going on?"

"I should have known, really. She's a Chronomancer," I said, still breathless. "I don't know anything else, but Aunt Vanessa's right: the real Jennet Device isn't a black eyed little girl, she's an adult woman and she was a Chronomancer."

I could see the wheels turning in Danny's brain again. He frowned.

"Nice one," Danny said. "That makes it much more likely that magic ran in the family."

I felt a lurch as something came hurtling through time. Angry and careless, Jennet Device, the living, adult Jennet Device, travelled from the past and appeared in the middle of the cottage, forcing Aunt Vanessa to leap to one side.

Her clothes hadn't survived the journey well: in 1632, they'd been worn, but still intact. After forcing herself through four hundred years of unstable time, they were ragged and tattered. In better light, I realized she was beautiful, with shining dark hair and a striking face.

Shame she looked like she wanted to murder me.

"Oh my days…" Danny said. "I've never seen that before."

"Stop your bloody gawping," Jennet Device snapped. "When are we?"

Aunt Vanessa stepped forward, trying her best cheery smile to calm the situation.

"It's the 21st century," she said. "We're sorry if we interrupted you."

Then Jennet did something I'd never seen before: she reached out with her power and whipped up the storm of unstable time around her. To Danny and Aunt

Vanessa she probably faded in and out of existence. For me, she was standing in the middle of the most dangerous storm I'd ever seen. Eventually, time destroys anything. I'd never seen anyone who could use it as a weapon before.

"I've a mind to send you all to dust," she said. "But first, tell me one thing: why do you stink of the dead?"

Maybe my grandmother could control time storms, but if she could, she'd never mentioned it. The whirling vortex of time around Jennet could do anything: age one of us to dust, or just carry us off to some remote part of time and leave us there.

I watched time whirling around her. I couldn't help imagining Danny aging and turning into an old man in front of my eyes... or Aunt Vanessa vanishing back into being a baby. The earth around her grew grass, which then died. The stones on the ground turned into gravel, then sand.

"I'm so confused," Aunt Vanessa said. "We've been seeing a little girl—"

"But you knew I died," Jennet said, laughing. "I die in Lancashire Castle."

"How do you...?" Aunt Vanessa asked.

Jennet Device laughed again. It wasn't a happy laugh. It was the laugh of someone miserable enough to think the joke is on them. She flashed a smile full of gritted teeth.

"You think you're the first person to think of using a time wizard on the house of Jennet Device, the Witch of Pendle?" she said, sneering. "You're late. Ages late. They've all been – asking me this and that. I get accused and I go to prison. I die there. I've been told since I was twelve."

Aunt Vanessa's face fell at the idea of people from the future coming and going repeatedly. My heart sank.

"I'm sorry…" I said.

"Yet you stink of the dead," Jennet said. "So tell me what you're about, or I'll send you God knows where."

I looked at Aunt Vanessa. Her expression was pure panic. Danny backed away, his eyes locked on Jennet - the living, adult Jennet. His lips twitched as he probably cycled through the incantations he'd learned, trying to find one that might help.

That pretty much left me.

"Well," I said. "The thing is, you become a revenant. Little girl about this tall... black eyes, disturbingly huge and with brutal magic powers... although you're not so bad right now."

Jennet watched me. I tried not to look at my feet. The clouds were heavy, but the dawn was starting to show. Still, I didn't need to see through time to know that it was going to rain in a minute.

"I've seen the child," she said. "I thought she was a Changeling."

"We just need to know what she wants--" I started saying again.

Jennet cut me off with another bleak, miserable laugh.

Danny looked sideways at me, and licked his lips cautiously.

"She showed us a bit of the day they arrested your family," Danny said. "But she was here, not you."

Jennet's face curled into a sneer.

"No need to tell you," she said. "You can see for yourself. You can guess where she'll be."

I glanced at Danny, then back at Jennet.

"...the mound behind the house. Did you bury people there when they wouldn't have them in the churchyard?" I asked.

"Come to the hill," Jennet said. "Speak the Hail Mary and it will open. You'll have your answer there."

Chapter Fourteen

You'd think a fairy hill would have flowers growing over it or sticks covered in ominous runes, but all this one had was mushrooms: warped, tea-colored ones that stuck out like half-buried saucers.

"Here it is," Jennet said, her hands balled into fists. "Speak the Hail Mary and it will open. Do you have iron?"

Danny nodded. He held up his hand to show her the ring. Jennet nodded approvingly.

"And do you have salt?" she asked.

I nodded. I'd snatched the tub of salt from the cottage's kitchen. After Connie had used it to make the circle, it was only half-full, but hopefully that would be enough. I took it out of my bag and managed to jam it into the big pocket inside my coat. They'd see it if they searched me, but hopefully it wasn't too obvious.

"Can anyone do the Hail Mary?" Aunt Vanessa asked.

Jennet nodded.

Aunt Vanessa stepped forward.

"Let me do it, then," she said. "It's my only chance to do a magical incantation. Anyway, if anything awful happens, I'd rather it happened to me."

Jennet smiled again. She stepped aside and waved Aunt Vanessa up to stand in front of the fairy hill. Dawn was coming on strong now, but the only thing that parted the clouds was a thin line of gold light on the horizon.

"Alright..." said Aunt Vanessa."Hail Mary, full of grace, the lord is with thee..."

The air split with the sound of moving soil. It wasn't like in the films; it was a deep, slightly wet ripping noise. The ground trembled under our feet and the fairy hill rose up into a vertical circle of mushrooms. The earth in the center dropped away, leaving a wide, dark tunnel.

"Go alone from here," Jennet Device said. "I can't enter the hill."

"Are you scared of meeting her?" Danny asked. "Your future self?"

Jennet gave him a look of irritation, and then vanished. I watched her slip back into her own time and stalk back to the house.

"I think that qualifies as a 'yes'," Aunt Vanessa said.

I kept watching the past as Jennet vanished into Malkin tower.

"If that's true," I said. "It's no wonder she became a revenant. If time travellers told me I was going to die every month for twenty years, it would do something to me."

"Yeah," Danny said, and pointed at the open hole. "Shall we?"

Stepping into the hole was like stepping into a gullet: the soil closed around us and pushed quickly into the earth. Aunt Vanessa screamed as it snapped shut, plunging us into the earth.

We travelled deep enough for me to feel very, very trapped. At best, we were going to be thrown out into a cavern deeper underground than the deepest tube station, with no escape. There were probably many Chronomancers, and a few badly-teleporting conjurers, who'd ended their days trapped underground.

I was just about ready to start screaming when the earth spat us out and we fell from floor to ceiling. I landed hard, feeling every kilo of my weight as I hit packed earth and carpet. Danny and Aunt Vanessa landed next to me, Danny jumping to his feet before either of us had had the chance.

"Greetings and well met," said a voice.

I recognised it, but I still lay on the carpet for a second, pretending to be stunned. The cavern was full of expensive things: fine wooden tables decorated with gold and beautiful silk hangings with gems sewn into them. The dim light came from coloured glass lanterns suspended from gold chains.

The dog spirit was standing at the other end of the room. He looked different down here: his muzzle and ears were sharper, and his eyes were dark red. It might have been a different talking dog-spirit, to be fair, but I doubt it.

"I know you…" I said, getting to my feet.

"What brings you here?" the dog asked.

"Jennet Device," I said. "When she was alive, not now. Your sister."

The dog growled. There wasn't anything human about its face but I could tell it was growling more from regret than anything else was.

"I betrayed her," the dog said, and dropped its head. "And she betrayed everyone else. I don't know what you think you're going to do."

"So, where's Connie?" I asked.

The dog padded backwards, shaking its head. If a human did it, you wouldn't think twice. From a dog, it was the weirdest thing I'd ever seen.

I hadn't really been feeling anything about losing Connie until then. After the river, something inside me had switched off. The only thing I'd been able to think was 'go here, do that, find the answers.'

Suddenly all the feelings came rushing back. Anger welled up like fire. We'd seen a man share his body with a demon once. A part of me wondered if that had been how he'd felt.

I took my iron ring and touched it to one of the glass lamps.

The dog flinched as the lamp stopped being glass and gold and became a candle in a tin can, hung from rusty chains. I put a tiny bit of salt in my hand and dropped it onto the carpet. The beautiful Persian rug turned into a filthy square of sewn-together sackcloth.

"I know what you are now," I said. "You've been kicking me around all day. You have my friend, you've nearly killed me, and you've made me ride across half of Lancashire on a stupid mountain bike. You can keep us down here, but if you don't start answering some questions, I'm going to start breaking things."

The dog lowered its head further, snarling.

"You'll die down here," it said. "All I have to do is nothing. Without me, you have no way out."

"Oh yeah?" I said. "One more thing.. I feel stupid talking to a dog."

I could feel the revenant magic lashing around the room, but he wasn't strong enough to affect us while we were wearing iron. The dog wavered like a reflection on water, but kept its shape as a dog. It snapped at my hand, forcing me back.

I tapped Danny on the shoulder.

"Did you get the horseshoe from over the barn door, mate?" I asked.

Danny smiled and took it out of his pocket.

"Iron," he said. "I wonder what'll happen if we touch you with this?"

The dog snarled, and then changed. From being a crouching, snarling black dog, it became the Parish Constable, Henry Hargreaves. He looked ragged and hungry, with jet black eyes. The only new looking thing he had was a sword strapped to his hip.

He drew the sword and put it between himself and Danny.

"Well that's a surprise," I said. "I thought you were just a ghost pulled out of the past."

"This is sharp enough to cut you," Hargreaves said. "Any of you. I don't want to hurt anyone, but if needs must…"

He swung the sword to point at me, then Danny again.

"Yeah?" Danny said. "What about this…"

Hargreaves touched the tip of the sword with the horseshoe. Nothing happened.

The revenant sneered and slashed at Danny, who yelped and jumped backwards.

"Oi!" he said.

Danny kept hold of the horseshoe. Fear flashed in his eyes as beads of blood trickled down his hand where he'd been cut.

"Oh lord," Aunt Vanessa said. "Danny!"

I poured a pile of salt into my hand. Hargreaves snapped the sword towards me.

"Stop," he said, taking a step forward. "You can take my magic, but this sword is real, and I've been doing this for a long time. You could all three attack me and I'd cut all three of you to pieces."

I should be honest, most of the time I'd have been frightened, but I was still angrier than I'd ever been. I'd never understood what people meant when they described anger like a red mist, but I had it. I'd been beaten, drowned and forced to go on a cycling holiday. Someone was going to pay.

I lunged forward and got under his blade. Aunt Vanessa yelled with surprise, which distracted Hargreaves long enough to let me slam into his side, head first, knocking him to the floor.

He smacked me on the side of the head with the handle of the sword. Pain and flashing lights exploded in front of my eyes. He used his sword hand to punch me in the face, then put his foot into my stomach and levered me away as hard as he could.

I jumped up, still slightly stunned from being hit, but still angry enough to fight. I wondered if I could slow time enough to dodge past his sword and hit him again.

"Esteban, stop!" Danny shouted.

"Yes," said Hargreaves, breathing hard. "Talk some sense into your friend."

"Esteban, mate, there's a better way," Danny said.

The revenant's smile faltered, but he kept his sword on me.

Danny bit his lip, untying and retying his dreads.

"Alright, Mist Hargreaves, I – that is to say, we – challenge you to a battle of riddles. Three riddles, set by you and answered by us," Danny said. "No violence. No cheating. If you win, you get what you want, whatever that is. If we win, you tell us where Connie and that creepy little girl is. You don't want to fight, we don't want to fight. We can do something else if you want, but we settle this with a game."

Hargreaves pointed his sword at me.

"I want him," he said. "If I win, you leave Pendle but the fat one stays with me."

I started to shake my head, but Danny caught my eye and nodded.

"Alright," I said, hoping Danny had a plan. "What about Connie?"

"I will do what I can," Hargreaves said. "She is the bait. You are the target. If you leave, Jennet will have no need of her. Mayhaps I can persuade her to be merciful."

"What does she want?" Danny asked. "Why are still

helping her?"

Hargreaves smiled sadly.

"To the second question, I help her because it is my punishment," he said. "To the first, I shall tell you if you win."

"We'd better win, then," I said.

Hargreaves stroked his beard and watched me.

"From the start of this I have designed to protect you," he said. "With my teaching you could be something great. But no matter. On your mark, we shall begin."

I got to my feet. Aunt Vanessa had found a cloth to wrap Danny's hand in, although it was already red with blood. Danny was trying to keep his cool, but I couldn't help noticing him look at the bandage every few seconds.

"It'll be alright," Aunt Vanessa said, quietly. "It wasn't too deep."

Danny nodded, and looked up at the revenant.

"Alright mate," he said. "First riddle. Let's have it."

Hargreaves stroked his beard and settled back into a rich ebony seat with a purple velvet cushion. I couldn't help wondering what it would look like without his power of illusion. He poured himself a glass of wine and sipped it thoughtfully.

"Very well…" he said. " In youth, I am slim and of height, but when old, I am small and stubbed. Pray, what am I?"

Danny looked at the bandage on his hand. I'd never seen him like this. Suddenly, I had a feeling that I was going to be doing this without his help.

"Danny mate," I said. "This would be a really good time for you to exercise that Conjurer's self-discipline you're always talking about."

"Yeah," he said, nodding. "'Course mate… wow, that's a lot of blood…"

Aunt Vanessa patted his shoulder.

"It's alright," she said. "It's not that bad, honestly."

Hargreaves smiled.

"If you intend to take some time, I could call for refreshments?" he said.

"No," I said. "You're alright. We could probably do with some clean bandages, though. Real ones that won't turn out to be rags and masking tape."

Hargreaves nodded and waved his hand.

"On the cabinet," he said, pointing at where a completely ordinary first aid kit had now appeared. "Your mother can do it while you think on the answer."

"She's my aunt, actually," I said.

He smiled and sipped his wine.

"As you wish," he said.

"Yeah…" I said, and racked my brain from the answer.

I stared at the coloured glass lanterns, with the flickering candles in side. I stared at the reflection of the candle flame in the glass, trying to push the anger and panic out of my head and concentrate on the question. In the corner of my eye, I could see Danny turning deathly pale as Aunt Vanessa used skin closures on his cuts so that she could bandage them.

"So, what's long and thin when it's young and short and fat when it's old?" I asked.

The image of one of my elderly Spanish cousins popped into my head. I'd seen pictures of Auntie Crisann from when she was young, and she'd been tall and thin. Now she was a bent little old lady who smiled a lot.

Then again, I didn't think the riddle would be based on a bad joke about the elderly. I watched the lamp light reflect off the gold decorations. Something occurred to me.

"Hang on," I said. "You didn't say short and fat. You said small and stubbed…"

I looked at the lamp again. Something fell into place in my head.

"It's a candle," I said. "A candle. It starts out long and it gets thinner at the top, then by the time it's burned down all that's left is the stubby bit at the bottom."

"That's right," Hargreaves said, smiling. "Alright, now for the next: after their grandmother was arrested, the Device women sat together for supper. Two mothers and two daughters sat at the table, yet all they ate were three small loaves and three fishes. How could this be?"

"Well, that's easy," I started saying. "Someone just didn't—"

"Esteban!" Aunt Vanessa said. "Think."

"Yeah," I said. "Alright."

I looked over at Danny. Aunt Vanessa had finished bandaging his hand, but he was still paler than I'd ever seen him. He'd sat on the ground with his eyes closed.

"Can we have it again please?" I asked.

Hargreaves smiled and took another sip of his wine.

"Of course: two mothers and two daughters sat to eat supper together. Each ate a meal of bread and fish, and yet only three small loaves and three fishes were eaten. How could that be?" he asked.

"Of the Device family?" Aunt Vanessa asked.

Hargreaves nodded.

"Just as you say," he said.

"And you're being specific?" Aunt Vanessa asked. "You mean the Device family as we know them from the Pendle Trial?"

The fairy nodded again. His smile slipped.

"Aye, as you say," he said, looking less amused this time.

Aunt Vanessa looked at me.

"I think I have this one," she said.

"Don't let me stop you," I said, motioning for her to get on with it.

She turned towards Hargreaves with her hands on her hips.

"There were two mothers and two daughters at the table, but only three people. One was Elizabeth Device, daughter of Mother Demdike – old Elizabeth Southerns – while the second was Elizabeth's daughter Alison. The last of them was Alison's daughter Jennet which meant two mothers and two daughters but only three people. That's your answer, that's how it was done," Aunt Vanessa said.

Hargreaves watched her expressionlessly. He threw the rest of his wine onto the floor with a flick of his wrist and slammed the goblet down hard on the table. If looks could have killed – which they might have if we hadn't been wearing iron rings – Aunt Vanessa would have been dead.

"I like beer better anyway," he said. "You are, of course, correct. And for the next."

Aunt Vanessa's smile grew. The relief deflated her a little.

"Alright," she said, glancing sideways at me. "Ask away. If nothing else, two out of three isn't bad."

"Very well," Hargreaves said. "For the last I shall say it only once. Speak and I speak but questions I will not answer. I speak in your every language but I understand not what I say. I shall cry out if you raise your voice, but fall silent and I will say nothing. What am I?"

"'Speak and I speak, but questions I will not answer...'" Aunt Vanessa said. "'I speak in every language but I understand not what I say... I shall cry out if you raise your voice, but fall silent and I say nothing...?'"

"Nothing?" I asked, trying to think.

"Nothing," Aunt Vanessa said, quietly.

"Nothing," Danny whispered, trying to shake himself out of shock.

Hargreaves watched us. He was trying his hardest to look like he'd sunk back into the cushion, but he'd moved so that he could jump up at any second. His hand rested lazily on his sword. I looked between Danny and Aunt Vanessa. Danny was getting himself back together, but he was still in a bit of shock.

I looked back to Hargreaves.

"Can we ask you a question?" I asked.

He shook his head, smiling humourlessly.

"No," he said, stroking his beard. "I say this only once."

Danny muttered the riddle, going over it repeatedly.

"Mate, stop it," I said, probably a bit more sharply than I'd intended. "The more you say it, the more you get bits wrong and it's confusing me."

Danny gave me a hurt look, and then hid it behind an easy-going smile.

"Fair enough," he said. "You anywhere near the answer?"

"Give me a minute," I said. "I've still got it going around and around in my he—"

The answer hit me. I grinned at Danny, who seemed to get there at the same time. Aunt Vanessa gave us a worried look.

"Alright," I said, turning back to Hargreaves. "The answer is an echo. It reflects sound back at me no matter what language I speak. If I speak, it'll speak and if I shout, it'll shout, but if I don't say, anything there's nothing to echo. That's the answer."

Hargreaves's face twisted into a grimace. He nodded unwillingly.

"Speak your requests," he said. "But be warned, I am only delivering you into greater danger."

"First things first," Danny asked. "She's powerful, why does she want Esteban?"

Hargreaves rolled his eyes.

"Do you not know?" he said. "She wants him to change the past. We can do a lot, but we cannot change anything."

"What does she want to do?" I asked.

Hargreaves shook his head, slowly.

"She wants you to change the past," he said. "As you have the power to do. As you might already have done."

He waved a hand and another hole opened up in the earth. A tunnel with loose dirt walls dropped steeply into the darkness.

"She's made her home over there," he said. "She's too strong for me. If you'd helped me before we did so much fighting, I might have overpowered her, but I'm too tired now."

I looked at Danny.

"We have to," I said. "We can't leave Connie."

Danny nodded, his expression serious.

I turned to Aunt Vanessa. She'd stuffed the first aid kit into her pocket and was standing ready to go through the tunnel.

"Come on then," she said, smiling. "Best foot forward."

I braced myself to travel down another tunnel.

"And so the trap is sprung," Hargreaves said, unhappily. "And the prey dance merrily into it."

Chapter Fifteen

This wasn't like the last one. I stepped through the hole expecting to fall deeper into the earth… and nothing. I stepped through into absolute darkness.

"Umm… Auntie Vee? Danny?" I called.

The darkness ate my voice. I would almost have preferred to be hurtling through the earth than to be hanging around in limbo. Then again, it was a sensible move if Jennet didn't want to fight us: she could just leave us alone in the dark and wait for us to starve. For a revenant who lived forever it probably felt like a fast solution.

I'd just thought about the tub of salt in my pocket when the room was flooded by light.

It would have been a grey, weak light if we hadn't been suspended in absolute darkness. A huge chamber opened around us. We weren't underground: the walls were grey plaster with white decorations. There were rails of dark brown wood on three circles descending into the middle, where Connie stood on a high wooden platform.

On the other side of the inner circle, two judges sat on high, throne-like seats.

"Have we travelled in time?" Danny asked, whispering.

I shook my head.

"No," I said, feeling around for time magic. "I think it's another illusion, like the carpet and the lamp in the other room."

Danny gave a low whistle.

"It's on a grand scale," he said. "I've never seen an illusionist who could make something like this."

"Revenants," I said. "Huge power, but with limitations. Anyway, this is the world of the dead."

Connie heard our voices. At some point, they'd given her her shades back, hiding the glowing pits that were her eyes.

There were four deep, angry looking, red scratches down the side of her face.

The judges noticed them at the same time as we did.

"Bailiff," said the first judge, looking around. "How has the prisoner come to this harm?"

We felt the world shift. Hargreaves appeared in the room, looking frightened and defeated.

He looked at us helplessly, then back at the judges.

"Well, you see, sir, some of the men – superstitious sorts – thought they should… scratch her, sir… to remove her powers, Justice Bromley, Your Honour," Hargreaves said.

The first judge, Justice Bromley, was a middleweight man, totally lost under his huge wig and his ornate red robes. The second judge, who had a bushy beard, looked on accusingly.

"Are your men aware, Mister Hargreaves, that such things are superstitious and illegal?" the bearded judge asked.

"Oh yes, Your Honour, Justice Altham," said Hargreaves, nodding frantically. "But they did so while I was dealing with matters of my office and there was nothing I could do nothing to prevent it."

Justice Bromley made a rumble like an oncoming storm.

"Mmmm? And did it work? Have her powers faded?" Asked Bromley.

Hargreaves squirmed uncomfortably.

"Well, sir, she hasn't escaped…" he said.

Bromley's face turned reddish-pink. For a minute, I thought his eyes were going to bulge out of their sockets.

Then another voice cut through proceedings.

"Your honour," said the voice. "I think a good deal of doubt can be laid to rest by requesting this court to remove the young lady's eye coverings."

"And here it begins," Altham said. "Mister Nowell would have us believe that every ague of the eye and pock on the skin is evidence for league with Satan."

The man who had been speaking stood up. He was tall, with a thick black beard and longish black hair. Fierce blue eyes glittered in his face. He gave the judges a clipped bow.

"Speak as you will, Your Honours," said Nowell. "Though I am aware that in the York Sessions just past, you have seen a body that bled most unnaturally at the touch of its murderer."

Althman looked unwillingly at Bromley, who inclined his head in agreement.

"Very well," said Bromley, looking at Connie. "Mistress, if you should agree to remove your eye coverings, this court should be much obliged."

Connie turned away from us and looked back at the judges.

"I'd rather not," she said. "But if you insist…"

She bowed her head and took off her shades. She stood, head bowed with her eyes closed. Her eyelids stretched over hollow eye sockets, but you could see the light from behind them.

Altham leaned out of his chair to try to see her properly.

"Please, Miss," he said. "It would oblige me if you should raise your head and open your eyes."

"If you insist," Connie said. "But take a deep breath and try not to panic."

She opened her eyes. White light shone into the room. Altham gasped. Bromley looked surprised, but composed himself and tried to keep the expression off his face.

Bromley looked back to Nowell. I was quite impressed that he still managed to look sceptical.

"You have something on the face of it," he said. "Where is this witness you claim?"

Danny tapped Aunt Vanessa and me on the shoulder.

"We should break this up," he said. "Where's Jennet?"

"Just wait," Aunt Vanessa said. "This should be where she comes in."

There was a rattle of chains. Two bailiffs, ones

I vaguely recognised from before, led Jennet into the courtroom. She looked around with black eyes. Hargreaves crossed himself, but none of the others seemed to notice.

"Even for her, it must be hard to do all this. I don't care how strong revenants are. Nobody can do it forever... in fact... I've got an idea..."

"Your Honours," I said. "If I can interrupt?"

One of the things about time magic is you get to meet some famous dead people. During a major crisis in London I met the King of England and Sir Christopher Wren. After that, I'm not scared of important people from the past. Particularly ones who are only projections of magic.

"Your Honours?" I said more loudly, climbing over the rails between me and the middle of the court. "Can I ask something please?"

They didn't react. I climbed right into the middle and stood in front of where they were sitting, waving my arms.

"Your Honours? Justice Bromley? Justice Althman? Can I say something?" I said.

In the dock, Connie leaned over and hissed at me.

"Fawkes," she said. "What in blazes are you doing? This is all just a projection. These people aren't real; she's stage managing it all."

I turned to Connie, laughing.

"I know, that's the pathetic thing," I said. "She's gone to all this trouble and she can't even get the real people. I thought she was an unstoppable revenant.

She's just a waste of space."

Roger Nowell, or Jennet's illusion of him, sneered.

"What is the meaning of this?" he asked, his hand balled around a sheaf of papers.

I forced a laugh.

"Shut up," I said. "You're not even the real thing."

I wouldn't have thought it was possible, but the little girl's eyes darkened. They stopped shining and turned into black pools in her face.

Nowell changed. A shorter, less good looking, less well dressed, less blue-eyed man appeared in his place.

I looked him up and down, forcing a cocky smile onto my face.

"So is this the real Roger Nowell?" I said, taking a step back. "He doesn't look like much."

Up in the gallery, Aunt Vanessa shouted down.

"He's right," she said, pointing at the little girl. "This court is almost empty: look at the witness box. How many people were there on the day? Have you forgotten about Jennet's mother?"

The girl turned to Aunt Vanessa, glaring viciously. Time shifted and churned.

Suddenly the dock was full: men and women, filthy and in iron. Alison Device, Jennet's mother, saw her and burst into wailing tears.

"Jennet," she sobbed. "Why are you doing this?"

The little girl looked between her mother and Nowell, who looked at Hargreaves.

"Will you just stand there, man?" Nowell said. "What is the meaning of this?"

Hargreaves looked at the little girl.

"You wanted this," he said, surprisingly kindly. "I've helped you get this far, girl. It's now or never."

Nowell's mouth opened and closed. He clutched his sheaf of papers as if his life depended on it.

I looked over at Hargreaves.

"I thought you wanted to stop her?" I asked.

Henry Hargreaves, Bailiff of Newchurch, shook his head.

"No, young master. I don't hold with some things, but what Mister Nowell did wasn't right. It wasn't justice."

"I don't understand…" I said, starting to feel my grip on events slip.

"He kept me in his house for months," Jennet said. "Mostly in irons… I couldn't stop him. After a while, I just did what he said. I didn't come into my magic till years after."

Roger Nowell's face contorted into a mask of fear. Around us, the courtroom flickered in and out of existence, and then vanished entirely. Time warped and settled as she let people slip back into the past.

Hargreaves looked between us, and then vanished.

It was just us, Jennet, and Roger Nowell, JP for Pendle Forest.

"God no…" he said.

He crossed himself, then looked angry and clutched his hands behind his back.

"Oh foul creature of hell," he said, and stepped back from Jennet. "Get thee back from me."

Now the illusion of the courtroom was gone, we were in a chamber a lot like the one Hargreaves had lived in, but bigger and full of coloured lamps and rich carpets. Some of them might have been real. Rough earth walls and bits of stone surrounded us. We were too deep for tree roots.

Nowell stumbled back in panic.

"Lord preserve me," he said. "Am I to die in the clutches of witches?"

"Why do you want this?" I asked.

The little girl looked at me.

"I couldn't help them," she said. "But I could have stopped it from getting worse."

I nodded. It was starting to make sense.

"They were witches and sorcerers of the Devil," Nowell shouted.

"They cured cows and horses," Jennet shouted back. "You murdered them."

Her chains vanished and her clothes changed: she wore a dress of white and green, with a corset, and a huge skirt. She was taller, too, almost as tall as Connie was.

Danny and Aunt Vanessa stepped into the middle of the room, watching the little girl cautiously.

"Why are we here?" I asked. "You could have done this any time."

Jennet shook her head.

"No," she said. "Because I can't change things. Whatever I do, whatever magic, everything goes back to the way it was next morning."

She reached behind her back and produced a long, sharp looking knife. Jewels sparkled and glittered in the hilt. Nowell's eyes bulged.

"You're a time magician," she said, holding out the knife. "If you do it, it'll stick."

"Esteban…" Aunt Vanessa said.

I thought about what my grandmother would do.

She'd probably decide what was right, do it without changing her mind, and not regret it.

Maybe I'll never be as good a sorcerer as she is. I looked at the others. Danny shook his head, barely noticeably. Connie really looked like she wanted to see the knife sticking out of Roger Nowell's soft bits. She put her dark glasses back on, blotting out the flickering white light.

"Feeling lucky Roger?" Connie asked. "If it was my choice you'd already be bleeding."

Nowell looked at them. He was breathing hard. Beads of sweat ran down his face. I tried to remind myself of what he'd done to the witches of Pendle before I felt sorry for him.

"Look," I said to the revenant. "Connie would do it. Maybe a dozen other Chronomancers would do it without a second thought… but I can't do it. I'm not going to do it."

Her dark eyes blazed with anger.

"He killed—" she said.

"I know," I said, interrupting. "But he's dead. You became a revenant and he's gone. Hundreds of years have passed and he's gone to dust. You've had to snatch him out of time and bring him here to do this. How much time will you steal from him? Twenty years? Thirty? It's nothing. It's already happened naturally. He's gone. What could you have done with the centuries of time you've had if you hadn't been doing this?"

She faltered. For the first time, I could see she wasn't certain what she wanted to do.

"The first thing you learn in time magic is that even if you can change things, you shouldn't," I said. "The past is always someone's future. There are time magicians three hundred years from now: how would we like it if they came back and messed with things because they thought it was right?"

Nowell watched us, breathing like he'd run a marathon. He slipped a tiny, stubby bladed knife out of his sleeve. It looked like something you carried to cut tobacco for a pipe.

"Look at him," I said. "He's desperate: ready to attack an immortal revenant with a tobacco knife."

I half expected her to do something when she saw him with the knife, but she didn't. She looked at it with more tiredness and disappointment than anger.

"I know," I said. "He was supposed to be your super villain nemesis but he's just a frightened old man with a little knife. It's probably not even sharp enough to hurt a mortal, being honest."

Jennet stumbled back and sat on a sumptuous ebony seat with a velvet cushion. She stared at Nowell for a moment, with her hand on her mouth.

"What do I do if I let him go?" she asked.

"Ask your friend in the other room," I said. "Anyway, you can't change things permanently, but people don't have to know that. There are many cruel, corrupt, prejudiced people out there in the world. I think it might be quite cool if they started saying, 'You need to be careful, or the dead might find out, and you don't want to mess with them…'"

The fairy woman looked at her hands.

"If I go on, I can't be Jennet," she said.

I shrugged.

"I don't know, what would you want? What would you want to bring to people?" I asked.

She looked up, looking at Aunt Vanessa and my friends.

"Hope," she said. "I'd like to bring hope."

"Good move, Hope," I said. "Let him go, eh?"

Jennet-now-Hope trained her iciest look on Nowell, who looked like he might have made a mess in his expensive black breeches.

"Go now, mortal," she said. "And know that you are already dead. You have been dust for centuries. If your God exists, I suspect he has a warm place prepared for you."

Nowell looked equally frightened and angry – then he vanished.

I let myself relax, just a little.

"Okay," I said. "I think we're all doing very well here. Why don't you celebrate by returning all of us safely to the surface?"

Chapter Sixteen

After that, things took a turn for the worse: Connie helped Aunt Vanessa repair the farmhouse, and we spent the rest of the weekend Mountain Biking.

Hope stayed around for a while, which was weird at first, but I got used to it. She managed to apologise for chasing, beating, and nearly drowning me during my first twenty-four hours in Lancashire.

I persuaded her to make an illusion of me that would go mountain biking so that we could sit in the warm and drink tea. I think Connie realised it wasn't really me, but she didn't say anything.

I sat with a revenant and watched Sunday telly.

"How long have we been watching this?" I asked.

"About ten minutes more than you last asked," she said.

"It's in black and white. Have we got to watch it?" I asked

On the TV, some brave pilots sent other pilots spiralling down to their fiery deaths. One of them made a mistake and got someone killed, and then someone wrote a poem about it.

"I'd like to…," said Hope.

I knew that tone. That tone meant, 'yes, we'll watch this if it's the last thing I do, but I'm too polite to say so.' I decided to let it go. If my powers of persuasion weren't working, experience suggested that force wasn't going to be a winning tactic.

It was then that I noticed Hargreaves, standing outside the house. A cold lump of dread formed in my stomach.

"Hostia…" I said.

My iron ring was on the other side of the house. Hope had persuaded us to put the salt securely in a high cupboard because it made her nervous.

Of course, it made her nervous.

Hope put a hand on my shoulder.

"It's alright," she said. "He wants to talk. He won't come in."

I looked at her. She'd changed into a green and white tracksuit. I tried to see if I could spot Danny and the others in the fields, but there was no sign.

I was too tired to be frightened.

"If this was part of some evil plan, you did it really well," I said. "You totally got me."

"I'll stay here," she said. "I'll fetch down the salt if you'd like me to."

I shook my head.

"That's okay," I said, pushing myself up. "I'd better go and talk to him. If you really wanted to hurt me there wouldn't be much reason to keep being nice to me like this."

Unless, I thought, there's something I don't know.

I went to the back door and opened it. Hargreaves stepped closer – just enough so that we could talk without shouting at each other.

"I admire what you did for us," he said.

"Um, thanks," I said, as silver tongued as always. "Your riddles were good. Now I understand why my grandmother makes me practise that sort of stuff."

"She's a wise woman," he said. "Give her my respects."

We stood in silence for a minute. He must have realised that I was about to make an excuse and shut the door in his face.

"Please," he said. "A moment. You have encountered things that should not be here, and you have accepted us as things that should. I appreciate that. I thought it good to say that should you require our help, and if there is anything we can do, you need only speak my name."

"Right…" I said. "Thanks, likewise, although it might take a while."

Hargreaves nodded, and vanished.

I spent the rest of the time having a weird but nice afternoon hanging out with one of the vengeful undead. After a while we phoned for takeaway and paid with illusory gold, but only because the nearest Macdonalds was in Blackburn.

After my first day in Lancashire, karma probably owed me.

Also by this author:

Great Fire

Jon Chant

The streets are paved with magic

Esteban Fawkes is a young sorcerer special-
ising in time magic, known as Chronomancy.
Danny is a Conjurer who can summon super-
natural beings, or banish the
Things That Should Not Be Here. When Danny
goes missing, a raging fire threatens to
engulf London. Aided by a bystander called
Connie, Esteban must travel back to Pudding
Lane in 1666 and battle the dark forces that
are threatening the city.

ISBN: 978-1906132309   UK: £7.99

http://www.mogzilla.co.uk/greatfire

About the author

Jon Chant is a London based writer who also works as a tour guide at Shakespeare's Globe Theatre. John's company specialises in guided walks around the spooky and macabre sites of London.

Jon has an uncanny feel for all things 17th Century and he has walked every inch of the backstreets and alleyways he describes in his first book - *Great Fire*.

Jon Chant writes fiction (and non-fiction) for adults and children and he has particular interest in the history of magic.

HAYWIRED
Alex Keller

Ludwig von Guggenstein is about to have his unusual existence turned inside out. When he and his father are blamed for a fatal accident during the harvest, a monstrous family secret is revealed. Soon Ludwig will begin to uncover diabolical plans that span countries and generations while ghoulish machines hunt him down. He must fight for survival, in a world gone haywire.

ISBN: 9781906132330   UK: £7.99

REWIRED
ISBN: 9781906132347

http://www.mogzilla.co.uk/haywired

Order
of the
Furnace
By Alex Keller

The Kingdom of Eltsvine is falling apart...

'An exciting, rip-roaring, action packed book set in a time and place where fantastical machines exist alongside humans. The squires (made up of boys and girls) in the Order of the Furnace are young but they are treated equally, are valued, trusted and more than capable of fighting alongside the adults. The snappy chapters are full of intense danger and activity. The amazing war engines, apparatus and animalistic soul-machines add a zip of steampunk to proceedings. The story rockets along, with buckets of bravery needed by the squires in order to survive the skirmishes set in their way. A fabulous start to a thrilling new series that should appeal to boys and girls (and some adventurous adults too) - long live *The Order of the Furnace!*'
Lovereading4kids

ISBN: 9781906132316

By Robin Price & Paul McGrory

This is a terrifically atmospheric page-turning adventure told through words and comic art. Set in the near future, in a flooded London where rival police forces – one for adults and one for kids – compete to keep the peace, it intertwines the story of Jemima, daughter of the Chief Inspector of Police, with contemporary issues of climate change and the environment in an original and provocative way but without sounding patronising. It's a rattling good read and one in which you are sure to be drawn in to Jemima's exploits of survival.' – www.lovereading.co.uk

ISBN: 978-1-906132-03-3

UK £7.99

www.londondeep.co.uk